The Fat Cat Fiddler at the [illegible] l

By the same author

Nerves, Worry and Depression: The Way Out, Dublin 1991

THE FAT CAT FIDDLER AT THE VATICAN BALL

John D. Nugent

GLENDALE

First published in Ireland
by Glendale Publishing Ltd.
4 Haddington Terrace
Dun Laoghaire
Co. Dublin

British Library Cataloguing in Publication Data

A catalogue record for this book is available
from the British Library

ISBN 0 907606 99 7

Typeset by Wendy A. Commins, The Curragh
Printed by Colour Books, Baldoyle, Dublin.

In gratitude to my brothers
Patrick and James Nugent,
who kept my boat afloat when the tide went out;
and, as always, with love for Maria
who stayed on board through stormy weather

*The characters in this novel are fictitious
and no reference is intended to anybody living or dead;
but the lachicos, go-boys and bad bastards
are entirely real, and deserve everything they get.*

Chapter One

My full name is John William O'Toole-Ball — my parents' fault, not mine. Nevertheless, I had an affectionate relationship with my mother who used call me 'Willy' and I had a happy childhood. It was different when I went to school. Boys can be very cruel and think nothing of shouting things on the upper deck of the 46A bus when one is coming home in the evening and the place is full of girls from St. Hilda's. In due time, a compassionate teacher re-christened me 'Jack', and I have refused to answer to anything else ever since. As I grew older, I quietly dropped the 'Ball' part of my surname, much to my father's chagrin as he was inordinately proud of his Anglo-Irish origins; but I felt I had suffered more than enough.

On leaving school I was placed with my Uncle's firm as a Solicitor's Apprentice. For ten years I toiled sullenly and learned so little as to render myself quite incapable of passing any examination. It was there, however, that I met Brannigan, a Law Clerk, with whom I shared a room. Brannigan spent most of his time either going out on messages to The White Swan — not the laundry — or leafing through an enormous file marked 'Fallopian Tubes (Ireland) Limited' and, shaking his head in mounting horror, whispering brokenly: 'Oh, Jesus, Mary and Joseph; God help us all.'

One summer my father eloped with my mother to get married and I have never seen them since. It was a turning point in my life. As my Uncle's auditors conducted their scrutiny most affably I was able to abstract a large sum from the clients' funds and establish myself as a Public Relations Consultant with a £100 Incorporation known as Image Erections (International) Limited — Jack O'Toole, President and Managing Director, Miss Cynthia Cockfosters, Director and Secretary, and one Augustus Brannigan, former Law Clerk, salaried employee and Legal Advisor to the company. To give ourselves some credibility in the business community and be like everyone else, we bestowed on each other honorary doctorates — a decision I came to regret, given the company in which we found ourselves. The enterprise plied its trade from one attic room on the fourth floor of 14 Guinness Row, in the City of Dublin. After two months of slack trading, the electricity was cut off and then adroitly restored by Brannigan who drove a six inch nail into the main and looped a metal coat hanger round the meter. The telephone never cost us anything as it had been left through at the behest of the Special Branch. This was due to Brannigan's hobby of making apparently subversive calls to imaginary contacts in the I.R.A. in furtherance of a plot to smuggle in six Jet Starfighters with nuclear warheads from a dishonest air crew in the United States Airforce (USAF—Russelheim), the agreed purchase money to be funded by a series of daring bank robberies, and some inside trading with a State-Sponsored body. Nothing more need be said of my past.

As to the present day, I spend a good deal of my time in the office when The Cart and Horse is closed; but mostly downstairs at the corner of the bar from which I can watch the halldoor in case a client should appear. Cynthia remains aloft during business hours to answer the phone and bytimes perform those little acts of kindness which are a solace to a lonely man.

If these papers fall into improper hands and, let us say, surface as a Seven Days Special on RTE, I will dismiss them as a work of fiction for I am about to detail a clandestine episode of international contingency in which Brannigan and myself played a salient part. We may now take up our tale in the intellectuals' corner of the Cart and Horse, where Brannigan and I were engaged in spirited argument.

I was not drunk but warmly aglow and well able to hold my own. Brannigan, being on that occasion a monied man, had been paying for the rounds as they fell due for consumption and was making the churlish point that natural justice demanded I might do the same from time to time. I, for my part, was advancing the cogent argument: 'Nemo dat quod non habet', a maxim from our legal days which freely translates as 'I can't pay my fucking round if I haven't the fucking money'. Brannigan, in reply, was enquiring why he should be the one who had to sign on to keep us in drinking money. I in turn enquired how I was expected to run a business if I was out all morning taking buses — the point being that if one were to sign on at Gardiner Street, Werberg Street, Blackrock and Dun Laoghaire under divers identities, some mode of conveyance was necessary to take one from place to place; the all round distance being not less than twenty five miles, be the same admeasurements more or less. Brannigan then hinted that he would have to consider his future with the company: a point I dismissed with levity as, whatever his human failings, his personal loyalty was beyond question. I then pointed out that as a company employee in I.E.I., it was his duty to discharge whatever tasks I, as President and Managing Director, might assign to him from time to time. Moving to the attack, I remarked stiffly that if he was really in earnest about coming on the board as a worker director, some initiative on his part must be shown and would he please explain why he had not thought of signing on at Cabinteely and Bray as well — a meagre addition of an extra hour's effort. Pressing my case, I shamed him into silence by observing that Cynthia – a delicate girl — was covering unemployment exchanges as far away as Trim, Navan and Kells. He had no answer to that and being a charitable man I said no more.

After some sulking, he brightened again and in more congenial tones asked me if I had seen the paper. I replied that I had — which was true as Christy had offered it to me at the bar — but I had been unable to read it due to poor light and double vision resulting from the night before.

'Ah, Jasus, 'tis gas,' Brannigan said, 'hasn't Delaney been caught again.'

By Delaney Brannigan did not intend to refer to that illustrious gentleman who brought honour to this country at the 1956 Olympics but to Hughie Delaney, boor, slob, gobshite in excelsis, the Minister for Civic Affairs. As Minister, Delaney was responsible for the conduct of An Bord Meow, The Cats' Board — a statutory body for the protection of stray cats — established at the directive of the E.C. from which the Irish Government took its orders. It appeared that the Bord had acquired a semi-detached site in Cabra for the erection of offices at a purchase price of £4.2 million. When this was noised in the media, a disagreeable furore ensued and questions were asked as to the identity of the Vendors who could command such a price for a semi-detached site in Cabra. It was further alleged that the site was wholly unsuitable for the construction of an office block large enough to accommodate the needs of the Bord, even though inspected prior to purchase by thirty-six auctioneers — party members all — at a modest fee of £20,000 per scrotum. Further probing revealed that the site had been sold to the Bord by a Jersey company called Pisspot Properties which then promptly bought it back for £3,600, in the name of Haemorrhoid Holdings, Cayman Islands. The Taoiseach thereupon announced his absolute confidence that the Bord had acted properly at all times but, ever the one for the highest standards, expressed the view that it might be proper if the Chairman of An Bord, the Minister's brother, Fonsie, resigned. Public blood lust seemed satiated for the time being and many there were who said that poor Fonsie had been very badly treated. An unsavoury London publication, *Private Eye*, then claimed that the principal shareholder in Pisspot Properties was none other than Hughie Delaney, the Minister. Civil Servants scurried from the Taoiseach's office buying up every copy of *Private Eye* but it was too late and by the time the evening papers were on the street the matter was public knowledge and with all the sanctimonious self righteousness which only a political opposition can display, outraged cries were heard for the resignation of the Government. Hughie Delaney, being absent on a private pilgrimage to Lourdes, was unavailable for comment; but on his return, issued a solemn and categorical assurance that he never heard of Pisspot Properties, had no interest therein, knew nothing of any site in Cabra or anywhere else and had only been informed of the existence of An Bord Meow that very morning. That was unwise. It is an axiom of Irish public life that nothing is to be believed until a politician gives a categorical assurance it is not so. The media screamed again and photocopies of the company returns were published showing beyond doubt that the principal shareholder was one Mhaire Ni Ickers, a Civil Servant and quite fortuitously, a cousin and Private Secretary to the Minister, the hereinbefore mentioned Hughie Delaney.

'Well, of course, that's the end of that,' I said.

'No, it isn't,' said Brannigan, swallowing the head of his pint in a nauseous display of gluttony, 'the Opposition are howling for his resignation.'

'Bullshit. They can't afford to bring the Government down and run the risk of getting into office themselves.' It is a fact of Irish political life that looderamawns and gobshites are to be found in equal numbers on all sides of the House and it is a foolish man who will stir out to vote; the running of the country being best left to the Civil Service who have always done their utmost under the most adverse of circumstances.

'Ah,' says Brannigan, warming to the point, 'hasn't Miss Nickers broken down and told all to a research student from U.C.D.'

'Oh sweet Jasus! Isn't it a fright to Christ that the perked, pensioned, and pampered politicians and Judges who are paid to guard the public interest can find out nothing while some poor bugger living on cheese and cream crackers can find out everything?'

My point was lost on Brannigan who, deep in the folds of his narrative, was mentally incapable of divided attention.

'Anyway, the Opposition has agreed to a Public Inquiry into the workings of An Bord Meow, which, of course, excludes any inquiry into the Minister's actions.'

'Which leaves Delaney over four million to the good.'

'Q. E. D.' said Brannigan. 'But isn't it a grand little country, just the same?'

And indeed it was, God bless it, but I was sorry to hear the end of the matter because there would be damn all to read in the papers but yet another serial about the fucking Kennedys until the next scandal broke. It was at that moment I espied o'er the rim of my glass, the fair Cynthia ushering a seedy cleric into the premises and advancing towards us in a diffident but business-like manner.

'This is Father Coddle, Jack,' she announced, 'he wants to see you.'

While the Irish clergy have never been behind the door when it comes to drinking their fair share — and, fuck the begrudgers, why should they? — it is unusual to see one of their number in licensed premises, not even in pursuance of their pastoral duties. Father Coddle was a small frayed person with a cheery face and, perhaps, the nervous demeanour of a drinking man who hasn't had a drink all day — the sadness being that the sun had long passed its zenith and was sinking towards evening. Nevertheless, he advanced courteously and thrust out his hand.

'So you're Jack O'Toole, are you?, he asked.

'Doctor O'Toole, if you please, Father. This is my associate Doctor Brannigan. I see you have already met my secretary, Doctor Cynthia Cockfosters.'

'Good, good,' he said warmly, rubbing his hands briskly, 'now what are ye all having?'

'My turn, Father,' I said graciously, 'I am in possession. Doctor Christy! An emolument of drinks, if you please!'

Christy bounded obediently forward rubbing his hands down his apron and Father Coddle and Cynthia seated themselves on adjacent stools.

'I think I'll go a large whiskey,' said his Reverence, a true son of his cloth.

'Vodka and lime,' said Cynthia quickly, in answer to a question I had not put.

'Same again,' said Brannigan, pushing his pint glass, white flecked and empty, forward on the counter.

'Ditto,' said I, Doctor Christy being fully aware of my abstemiousness and that even in extremis not a drop of alcohol will pass my lips unless it is a large gin and tonic, a slice of lemon and none of your ice only diluting good gin.

Father Coddle pushed back his sleeves and rubbed his hands again like a man who wanted to get down to business but didn't know how to begin.

'God, isn't it terrible cold,' he said.

'Brass monkeys,' said Brannigan. I rebuked him immediately with a stern glare.

'Desperate,' said Cynthia.

'Most intemperate,' said I.

And for some moments that seemed to be the sum of the conversation anybody wished to make. Father Coddle began again.

'Of course,' he remarked, 'it's September. No getting away from it.'

'The evenings are getting fierce short,' said Brannigan.

'Desperate,' said Cynthia.

'The season of mellow fruitfulness,' I said, making it plain that I had been to a good school and none of your counting up to ten or saying the Our Father in Irish and calling it an education.

Christy placed his laden tray on the counter and began to distribute the glasses in accordance with the stated preferences of the gathering. With all the deft dispatch of a conjurer he swept the empties away for onward carriage to the far end of the counter where he would clean them with a roller towel hanging on the yard door.

'Ah, then, God bless you,' said Father Coddle. He plunged his hand into his raincoat pocket. 'Here, let me pay for these.'

'Not at all, Father,' said I heartily, also sinking my hand and turning over again the two pence piece which nestled in the lining of my pocket. Due to the cut of my trousers, I had difficulty getting my hand out again.

'No, Jack, you're far too good,' said Father Coddle. He pulled from his breast pocket the largest wad of notes any of us had ever seen in our lives.

'Jesus Christ!' said Brannigan, his voice glued to the roof of his mouth.

'Will you watch your language in front of the priest,' I protested, greatly angered. If there's one thing I can't abide it's bad language or any kind of smut or filth. I was already suffering some degree of pressure from my hernia trying not to say 'fuck' in the presence of the holy man and I saw no reason why Brannigan should be allowed the full reign of eloquence while I had to stutter for words with the beads of perspiration rolling down my back — and I Managing Director of the company.

'Desperate altogether,' said Cynthia. Brannigan was, she obviously remembered, a mere employee of the company and not a director like herself and myself.

Father Coddle put a decent hole in his whiskey and smacked his lips. Then he turned to me.

'I hear, Jack, you're a public relations man?'

'Image Erections International Limited. I am the President and Managing Director.'

'I'm the secretary,' Cynthia put in.

'That will do, Cynthia. Now, Father, what's your problem?'

He rested upon me a long, speculative look.

'Tell me, Jack, would you be interested in taking on a most important and wide ranging commission?'

I pursed my lips thoughtfully and tilted my head to one side, allowing my eyes wander slowly up the mirror at the back of the bar, past the carved mahogany turrets over the top shelf and across the ceiling.

'By Christ he would!' said Brannigan before I had half

a chance to settle into my demeanour of mature consideration. I broke off impatiently.

'Look, Brannigan, like a good man; would you go up to the office and watch the phone.' I was minded to order Cynthia off the pitch as well but it occurred to me that as she was wont to get randy as evening came on, the prudent segregation of the sexes demanded that she shouldn't be closeted above in the Company headquarters with Brannigan.

'I better finish this,' Brannigan said.

'Bring it with you,' I said curtly.

'Desperate,' said Cynthia to no one in particular. I eyed Brannigan imperiously out the door; a subsidiary warning glance to Cynthia at the same time. I paused and took a cautious nibble at the edge of my drink.

'What did you have in mind, Father Coddle?'

'You haven't said whether you'd be interested,' said the priest mildly. I shrugged.

'Father, I'm a business man; a company executive. I am interested in any reasonable proposition which comes along.'

'Good, good,' cooed Father Coddle. 'You're a man of discretion?'

'Of course.'

'Good. Good. That's what's required. Tell me, Jack,' and he searched my face with no more than casual interest, 'do you say the odd little prayer at all?'

It is a sacred ethic of business that a good deal should never be lost for the want of telling even the most grotesque lie. But, as every politician knows, a good lie must always be credible. There is absolutely no point whatever in telling lies unless the other party is deceived.

'Well, now,' I said after mature consideration, 'I wouldn't describe myself as a religious man ... only be trifling with the truth ... fact is ... but heart in right place ... not quite at home with formal worship .....'

'You wouldn't be, say, active in the Legion of Mary, like?'

'Not really, but ....'

'Or the Knights?'

'Well, you see, Father, matter of money involved there, things a bit short recently ....'

'I know, I know. You wouldn't be identified with what we might call Catholic Action ....'

'Well, when I was at school ....'

'Or, let's say; you might miss Mass for a few months or two ....'

'Well, as I was saying, when I was at school ....'

'Oh, for God's sake, Jack, will you answer the quesion! Father, he doesn't go to Mass; he hates the Church, and he's always saying that if Jesus Christ was any good, he'd horsewhip the bastards out of the Vatican.'

'Shut up, Cynthia.'

'Ah, is that what he says, Cynthia? Ah, God help us; I often thought the same myself. Ah, dear, dear. The Church is a humble pilgrim, of course.'

I had had far too much to drink that day.

'Ah yes, bejasus,' I burst out despite myself, 'and when it suited ye, it was the Church militant, click the fingers and every head would bow. Now, bejasus, when that doesn't work any more, it's swing the altar round the other way and pimpled little farts with banjos playing what they think is rock and roll during Mass, and right wing reactionaries from Maynooth without a day's pastoral experience being imposed as Bishops — male, celibate, childless geriatrics telling the people what they can and can't do in bed.'

Father Coddle nodded serenely.

'Indeed, and that's about the size of it, Jack. Ah, God help us.' He shot me a quick, quizzical look. 'Do you know, you're a sound man, Jack O'Toole.'

Not knowing what to do or say, I downed the double gin in a gulp. Father Coddle motioned to Christy who was cowering down the bar and blessing himself at the double. He was certain that my outburst would bring a bolt of lightening through the ceiling. I repented at once of my discourtesy to this harmless priest.

'I wouldn't like you to think, now, Father, that I meant one word of that personally ....'

'Some of his best friends are priests,' put in Cynthia and while I detect interruptions while I have the floor, I noted for reference that Cynthia had a useful flair for diplomacy.

'Not at all, not at all, Jack. I agree with every word you say. Of course, you and I are but humble labourers in the vineyard and we'll pass no remarks on the antics of those who should know better. Isn't that the charitable and sensible way to look at it?'

As Christy had planted a newly polished glass sparkling with gin and tonic and a slice of lemon floating on the pool-like surface in front of me, I was well disposed to take a tolerant view of what Father Coddle had said — not that I could clearly remember what it was.

'I suppose so,' I said.

'Do you know who the biggest hoors of the lot were?'

'Who?'

'The twelve apostles!'

I blinked and subjected Father Coddle to a penetrating gaze. I inspected his collar and cloth closely. Could it be that he had been unfrocked for messing with parish funds or the ladies of the altar society? Had he, perchance, put in for his P45 to Rome and been held up like thousands of others by the bucolic intransigence of J.P. 2?

'The twelve apostles?'

'Ran off and left Him. The whole bloody lot of them. At the first sign of trouble. Fecked off.'

'The bastards.'

'There you are now. So you wouldn't expect too much from their successors; now would you?'

I had not been inside a church door since the year Wilbur and Orville Wright left the ground at Kitty Hawk, North Carolina nor have I been since but it did cross my mind that if Father Coddle represented the present day Church, maybe it had gone private since I knew it and the show had been placed in the hands of some bright spark like Fergal Quinn. Or maybe, I wondered suspiciously, Father Coddle was one of these trendy young rebels at loggerheads with his Bishop.

'Tell me something, Father Coddle. Are you carrying on with your housekeeper by any chance?'

'Desperate,' said Cynthia breathlessly. Father Coddle laughed until the tears filled his eyes.

'Jack, like a good man, would you ever come out with me to Dunfeckin and take one good look at my housekeeper. You'll see then why my celibacy is intact.'

'Have you notions of leaving the Church and writing a book about priests and nuns having it off in a confession box?'

'Ah, God help us. Any book I'd write wouldn't have much in it. No, Jack, I'm a priest, and don't blame the Church for that, for it's God's fault, and I like my job.'

God help him, I thought. He was a decent man, probably a saintly one. There was obviously no future for him whatever in the Church. But I was satisfied at last. I had no time at all for these loud young game cocks with the open necked shirts, who'd blow the foam off their pint on the floor and say 'Bollocks' every two minutes. And in no way could Father Coddle be held responsible for centuries of superstition and the pathological attitudes to sex and the persecution of women.

'OK, Father Coddle, you've got yourself a deal.'

He smiled and nodded and we shook hands on it. Then he lifted his glass, downed the last of his whiskey and stood up. He slapped the wad of notes down on the counter in front of me.

'There's the guts of a thousand pounds in that, Jack,' he said. 'Down payment on your retainer. Now I'll report back to my superiors and there'll be someone in touch with you shortly to discuss the matter further. To tell you the truth, I don't know what they want.' With a quick smile for all souls on board, a friendly nod and a retreating benedictional wave he was gone and Cynthia and I were left staring at the loot, neither of us fit to say whether the whole thing had been an alcoholic hallucination brought on by drinking out of damp glasses. Then, mindful of where I was, I pulled myself together. I stuffed the bundle into my pocket before Christy saw it and started making representations about reducing our overdraft on the slate. Jauntily I turned and looked into Cynthia's eyes which had become limpid pools of bottomless blue.

'We'll book into Jury's for the night and have dinner as well.'

'What'll I tell me mother?'

'Ring her later and tell her you missed the bus.'

'Desperate. I'll say I'm staying with Pauline. Look, Jack, Brannigan is owed two months wages. You'd want to hold on to a bit of that for him.'

'The blind bollocks! I'll give no money to any man who'd be saying "Jesus Christ" in front of a priest. Now, there's fifty pee. Go out and ring a taxi and tell them we want nothing less than a black Mercedes. None of their fucking clapped out Datsuns, now mind.'

Chapter Two

Morning will come, alas. In principle, I have no quarrel with that arrangement but I dislike being about before the streets are well aired. There are, as every drinking man knows, those barren, uneasy hours before the pubs open and people like me who are delicate in the early hours do not wear well if obliged to take to Capel Street and visit the early houses in the markets. It was a condition of our hotel room tenancy that we vacate promptly after the breakfast I was afraid to eat and earlier than was decent I found myself shivering at my desk; my head going like a jackhammer and my body featherweight as a child's balloon in imminent peril of floating up to the ceiling. Nothing availed.

'Will you go down in the name of Christ and knock on the window and ask him to let us in.'

Cynthia demurred.

'It's no good, Jack. He keeps shaking his head and pointing to the clock.'

'Bollocks!'

Mercifully, my back was to the morning glare from the window. To my right, at one end, Cynthia sat poised pro forma over her typewriter. In so far as I could see her, she looked flushed but well; her face in peaceful repose. At the other end of the desk Brannigan sat, the telephone cradled in front of his shoulder.

'How're ye fixed for chemical warheads?'

From the far end I could faintly hear an emphatic spluttering from his cousin Thady. Thady was a lanky teenage boy who never went to school but spent all his life in front of the television watching war videos. By dint of diligent listening through the years he had mastered to perfection every North American accent from Galveston to Gander and from Baltimore to the Barbary Coast. Brannigan, who brought to his role a potent reality, listened with mounting anger.

'That's no fucking use to us,' he stormed. 'A fucking firecracker from Moore Street would do better than that. It's either fucking chemicals or the whole deal is off.'

Once again an irritated paragraph crackled from the other end. Young cousin Thady had also a bright future in the dramatic arts.

'Ah, here,' snapped Brannigan, 'fuck that for a wanker's waltz. If ye can't supply the stuff, we'll do business with the Israelis.'

I gestured wearily.

'Enough,' I groaned.

'And three hours flying endurance is no fucking use to us either. Sure, Jasus, man, you'd hardly hit Buckingham Palace and Westminster and get back in that. Anyway, what about spare parts and after sales service?'

'Enough, Brannigan, for God's sake.'

'Lissen, I have to go for a piss. I'll ring you tomorrow.'

Wholly absorbed in his part, he slammed down the phone with a furious crash.

'Stupid American cunts!'

I covered my head with my hands.

'I wish you wouldn't use that word as a term of derision.'

If fantasy interweaves too closely with fact, it is difficult after a time to tell them apart. As I sat trembling in the chair, I struggled to remember the events of the previous night. Time and again my hand crept into my breast pocket for a re-assuring feel of the wad of notes. It was the only certainty — or, at least, tenable suspicion — I had that the Roman Church numbered amongst its priesthood, one Father Coddle. Otherwise the night had been a disaster. In the taxi from the hotel, Cynthia had proudly confided that she had come twelve times, dismissing my own count as a paltry three; but I had no memory whatever of these delights. The only tentative evidence I had was a stinging soreness in the Private Member which lay lifeless in the crotch of my trousers — of no standing in the community. Cynthia, by contrast, glowed with inner happiness.

Worse was to beset me.

'Listen, Jack, Cynthia says you have the few bob for me.'

I shot a scalding glance of Christlike reproach to the treacherous Cynthia. She met it unabashed.

'What? What few bob?'

'Oh, for God's sake, Jack. Give him his money and no more about it.'

'Come on, Jack. The mother is complaining. The wheelchair is in Meredith's this two months.'

I looked aghast from one to the other.

'Are you seriously suggesting that I as President and Managing Director of this Company engage in an asset stripping operation to hand out money to a man who neglected to sign on at Cabinteely and Bray?'

'Jack, for fuck's sake!'

'Suppose the creditors put in a Liquidator; do you seriously think I'm going to sit down in the High Court explaining that I handed out corporate assets to my closest friend while the company was insolvent?'

Brannigan drew his chair nearer and put his face discourteously close to mine. Cynthia said 'desperate'.

'Lissen, Jack, I don't give a fiddler's fuck for the High Court or the Low Court or the creditors or the company. I want my money.'

'I might manage fifty pounds on account. What about a promissory note under seal?'

'Money, Jack. Keep your fucking seals for the zoo.'

He was implacable in his avarice.

'Here's a hundred quid,' I said resignedly.

'And the other four, if you don't mind.'

I was too tired to reason with him further. He was a heartless, greedy man and quite unconcerned that I was being forced into a breach of the Companies Act. It's when things are at low ebb you know who your real friends are. In a post alcoholic despair I counted off from the slimming bundle. Then Cynthia's hand was out.

'Fifty pounds, please.'

'For what?'

'Me knickers. You tore them.'

The disgusting, shameless lie revolted me; and Brannigan, a mere employee of the company, standing there listening.

'How dare you!'

'You wouldn't wait.'

Brannigan's face twisted in a lascivious leer. It had come to that; the most intimate and sensitive matters were being brutally noised in the market place.

'There isn't a fucking knickers in Ireland worth fifty quid — even if there was a scintilla of truth in the dirty lie!'

''Tisn't Irish. 'Tis French. From Brown Thomaseses'. Do you want to see the cut of me bra after you?'

Terrified by the prospect of a further claim, I ripped off a fifty pound note and slapped it on the desk. Utterly wounded, I turned away in contempt. Cynthia snapped it up and drew her skirt up along her leg. She folded the note into the top of her tights. Brannigan's mouth worked manically and his eyes gleamed like a greyhound who sights the hare. Mournfully, my fingers went back into my pocket to assess the balance of company property. The bundle of notes, so recently plump and healthy, was now thinned disastrously. Any bulk which remained was made of singles. Why was it always my destiny to be surrounded by predators? However, as Managing Director, self pity was an indulgence and it behoved me to take a firm grasp on things. I opened as boldly as I dared.

'Was there a Father Coddle with us last night?'

They gaped at me.

'Of course there was. Wasn't it him what gave you the money?'

'What did he want?'

'He has a job for us,' said Brannigan. 'Us' if you

please. Puffed with money, he was now being forward enough to imply that he was a member of the company. I was in no state to argue but resolved to draw down the matter when — if ever — I felt better.

'What's the job?'

Brannigan shrugged and looked at Cynthia.

'He never said. he just asked if you were interested. He'd report back to his boss and someone would contact you in a few days.'

'It mustn't be much of a job if there's only a few hundred quid in it. Sure, Brannigan would draw more on a Friday.'

'Oh, there's better to come,' Cynthia explained. 'He just left you a thousand pounds on account. Running expenses, I suppose.'

'A thousand pounds! And, of course, with you crowd ripping me off, that explains why I've only about seventy left.'

'No, Jack. What about the room? What about the pheasant and the oysters and all the glasses of Fairy Liquid? What about the hundred you slipped to the waiter for cleaning up after you got sick all over the table? What about the few to the band to let you sing "Begin the Beguine?" Sure, you couldn't be stopped.'

'That's quite enough, Cynthia. You'd want to mind your drinking, you know. These delusions of yours are serious signs of brain damage.'

'God help you, Jack. And you sitting there not knowing the fuck whether it's November or July.'

I had no time for futile argument.

'Well, we'd want to get on to Father Coddle and tell him that if he wants to be serious about it, we better be put in funds.'

'I don't think that would be a good idea for a few days,' Brannigan warned.

'Why not? We can't run a major operation on buttons, you know.'

'You might have a point if you knew what he wanted.'

If there's one thing I despise it's loud mouthed, know-all hirelings standing about and giving lip and guff out of them while their betters are trying to concentrate on the serious issues at hand. There is only one way to silence uppity employees. Give them something to do.

'Look, go down to Christy and if he won't open up, at least let him hand out a few jars through the door.'

Brannigan shook his head.

'Won't work, Jack. We tried that last week.'

Cynthia wrinkled her nose.

'Ugh. I don't want a drink.'

Ungrateful bitch.

'I'll drink it, then.'

'Well, you won't,' countered Brannigan. 'He won't do it.'

With all the lofty contempt of a defeated General who has been deserted by his cowardly troops but will fight on alone, I rose with dignity and began a shaky progress to the door. They needn't think that when I had possession of the corner stool again, they could cluster around me like deprived orphans in the snow and expect me to succour their needs. My kindness had been exploited far too often. The floor creaked underfoot and I had the sickening impression that it was tilting madly from side to side.

The staircase, steep and narrow, twisted eerily down. Clinging bravely to the wall, I descended cautiously and paused to regroup on the landing below. Mrs. McGrath, an inquisitive woman, but a randy one given to entertaining the postman,put her head out the door.

'Ah, God love you, Mr. O'Toole; you're not well.'

'Doctor O'Toole to you, Ma'am; and I'm quite well, thank you.'

'Come in out of that and have a sup of tea.' Her robe parted and exposed a hairy, muscled leg in black sequins. I clenched my fists and tightened my throat against a surge of nausea.

'No thank you. I am quite well.'

'Ah, sure, don't I know what it's like. Jasus, if it wasn't for the valium I'd be on the drugs meself.'

I launched myself off the wall and down the nursery slopes. The cold breeze whipped up from the street and the glare from the hallway was merciless. With trembling fingers I drew a coin from my pocket and tapped furiously on the frosted glass of The Cart and Horse. I felt all the fever of a man taken short after a feed of senna pods who rushes upstairs and finds the lavatory locked. Compared to the lethal silence within, Dail Eireann during a parliamentary debate would be a riot of boisterous activity. But Christy's bicycle lay against the window.

'Christy! Christy! If you don't open up the fuck out of that, I'll let the air out of your tyres.'

No answer.

'Christy! I'm warning you, I know you're in there. I'm serious.'

Not a stir. Sunday in Belfast.

'Ah, please, Christy, please. God knows, I only want a mineral.'

The shafts of sunlight were spearing through my eyes and the icy street breeze was going up the legs of my trousers and curdling round my Jockey Y-Fronts. By some physical phenomenon which I could not explain I was both shivering and sweating at the same time. It crossed my mind that unless I got some nourishment into me I would collapse there and then on the street. There was little consolation in a moment's malicious enjoyment at the vision of Christy stammering and stuttering and trying to explain his hardness of heart to the City Coroner.

'Mr. Jack O'Toole?'

I jumped in my standing and swung around. Smartly uniformed in black, polished black leggings, peaked cap set square to the head, he stood at my elbow like a Nazi officer up for the Nuremberg Rally. The small pinched face seemed vaguely familiar. With a Herculean effort, I drew about me the tattered remnants of dignity.

'Doctor O'Toole, if you please.'

He nodded his head briskly to the sleek black limousine which stood purring at the kerb. It was inordinately long, the tinted glass making it impossible to see who, if anybody, occupied it.

'Monsignor Casserole wants to see you.'

Without waiting, and almost pulling me, he led me by the elbow to the car. The rear door swung open and somewhat bewildered I stepped in. The door closed behind me with an expensive clunk.

The ecclesiastical figure within sat deep in the cushions, his tapering fingers joined at the tips and set like a steeple propping up his lower lip which hung thoughtfully on his white fingernails. A pair of cold eyes regarded me with an opaque curiosity. Meanwhile the chauffeur had gone to the front, thrust his arm out the window and waved the peasantry back. With that, the car glided arrogantly out into the traffic and moved noiselessly down the street.

'Where are we going?' I asked indignantly. I had recovered my poise and was acutely conscious that the hour of opening was nigh. I had no time to spare motoring through the town at the whim of this insolent cleric.

'I am Monsignor Casserole, Secretary at the Nunciature.' The voice was dry, a breeze stirring in a cemetery.

'The what?'

'The Papal Nunciature.' I frowned.

'Is that the place above in the zoo?'

'The Phoenix Park.'

'The same thing. What do you want, Father?'

He had the polished, well fed, rounded cheeks of an intelligent rat, and a pair of small, liquid eyes which had never left my face. His clerical suit was tailored in expensive cloth, a pair of spotless white cuffs showing at the wrists. Gold cuff links gleamed on the white linen. There was a chilling smell of Holy Water in the car, but after standing in the scything cold of the street the luxurious interior was warm and hypnotically comfortable.

'We shall drive through the metropolis while we talk. I understand from Father Coddle that you are willing to undertake a delicate mission?'

'Look, Father, I don't want to be disrespectful; but I'm a very busy man at this time of day.'

He nodded impassively, stared at me for a moment, and then, with the gesture of a man going against better judgment, lifted an expensive leather brief case from the deep carpet at his feet. He passed over a long white envelope.

'Open it.'

The flap was embossed with an ornate crest; miscellaneous bunches of grapes and beribboned hats. Jack Horner-like, I stuck in my thumb and tore it along its length. I withdrew a bundle of notes, dirty, crinkled and well used. The denominations were large and varied. At least a few thousand, I thought.

'What's this?' I simpered, crucifying my face into an ingratiating subservience. A vision of many a gin and tonic standing in a long line of tall glasses and reaching to eternity entranced my inner eye.

'That is obvious, I should think.' He held out an immaculately manicured hand, faintly perfumed. 'The envelope, please? Thank you.'

'Further on account?'

He nodded coldly. With as much haste as was decent, I crammed the money into my pocket. Given that opening time was a matter of minutes away, it was heroic of me not to jump from the moving car but address myself to business.

'Now, Father, what can I do for you?'

'I understand from Father Coddle that you are not an ardent supporter of Holy Mother Church?'

The money was safely in my pocket, opening time was upon us; and there was no time to lose in semantics.

'I suppose you could say that.'

'And yet you are willing to work in her interests?'

'Look, Father, I'm in business. The Kremlin, British Intelligence, the Mafia, Charlie Haughey, the Church; if the money is good, what's the difference? I'm a businessman.'

'But are you a discreet one?'

'Of course. Why do you ask?'

'The mission is delicate and your health is in issue.'

'My health?'

For the first time he took his chilling eyes from my face and looked straight ahead, speaking softly as if to himself.

'The Church has many concerns which must be entrusted to outsiders; for reasons of discretion, you understand. You have heard of Signor Calvi?'

The name I had heard before but just at that moment I could not recall the connection. I shook my head.

'Signor Calvi,' he purred on, 'was an Italian gentleman to whom the Church entrusted a most sensitive enterprise. He became talkative.'

'Oh, I wouldn't do that.'

He stared impassively at me again.

'Indeed? Signor Calvi did. Signor Calvi died. I understand from those who witnessed it that his passing was a slow and most exquisitely painful one.'

Then I remembered. Signor Calvi, a prominent Italian banker, had been dealing in forged bonds for the Vatican. One sad morning in London he had been found hanging beneath the arches of Blackfriars bridge. I shivered to realise that the name of the bridge was singularly apt. I also recalled with increasing dismay that some of his associates had deemed it prudent to cast themselves from upper floor windows rather than take the more conventional way of reaching the street by descending the stairs. Monsignor Casserole turned upon me a flat, expressionless gaze.

'We understand each other?'

I nodded mutely.

'Excellent. And Mr. Brannigan and the girl, Cynthia?'

'Doctor Brannigan,' I gulped, 'and Doctor Cynthia are utterly reliable.'

'Excellent. You are very quick to take a point, Doctor O'Toole.'

I thought it better to re-assert myself.

'You would hardly have sought my services, Monsignor, unless you thought me a man of unusual calibre?'

A faint wintery smile showed briefly on his face; the gleam of candle light on the breast plate of a coffin.

'You are a fool and a drunk but a resourceful one. Your principle use is that you are deniable. Of course, being a fool and a drunk is one thing but being a dead fool and a drunk is quite another.'

I swallowed.

He leaned towards me, the corner of his mouth dipping sarcastically.

'I see no reason to continue this unpleasant conversation, do you?'

'You will find', I said with a valiant effort at recovery, 'that our services are well worth the money.'

'Of course.'

With a start, I realised that we were now proceeding into Guinness Row again.

'Now, Monsignor. What are the details of this matter?'

He looked at me again with expressionless distaste.

'His Excellency will see you in due course and outline the concerns of the Church. You will await instructions.'

He pressed a languid finger on a button by his side. A buzzer sounded in the chauffeur's glass-walled compartment. Abruptly, the car swept in to the footpath, a few paces from the door of the Fart and Arse, now legitimately open to admit those lawfully requiring refreshment and able and willing to pay for same. By some electronic means, the door beside me hissed open and the cold air of morning blew in. Monsignor Casserole's sensitive face twitched in discomfort.

'You will ponder in your heart', he said, 'my words as to the necessity for the utmost discretion.'

'You may depend ....'

With a disdainful gesture, he waved me away.

'Get out, please.'

I scrambled to the footpath and turned to make a respectful farewell. But the door swung closed in my face and with blatant disregard for the traffic flow, the car forged out again into the street amidst a sudden screaming of brakes and an indignant hooting of horns. Overcome by the encounter, I stood and watched it disappear down the street and then walked backwards, but unerringly, into the premises.

A fine dust hung in the air, glinting and falling in the sunlight. The boozy, night-before odour of stale cigarette smoke mingled tastefully with the tang of Jeyes fluid, Christy being punctilious about cleanliness in the premises. My eye was taken by the enormous bum of Mrs. McGrath, encased in a scarlet skirt and overflowing on a stool, her massive tits almost encircling the pint glass on the counter in front of her. It was Brannigan's considered opinion that she inflated her bosom with a bicycle pump every morning and she certainly cut a statuesque figure who carried it all before her; but only the postman would be in a position to verify Brannigan's theory, whatever other positions he might find himself in on his daily visits. But I was in no humour for lust. No redblooded man has a moment for such thoughts if there is need of serious drinking. I tore my eyes from her breasts and drank deeply from the tall glass Christy had brought to me.

'That's the hardy one,' Mrs. McGrath called out. I glanced quickly at my trousers but I was properly dressed. The second double gin was well inside me before I was capable of coherent thought. It was a comfort to know that the corporate assets of I.E.I. had increased dramatically, but, fortified somewhat, a choking indignation was welling up within me.

'A condescending, supercilious, Italian bastard,' I exclaimed.

'Probably be Pope one day so,' remarked Brannigan. I looked up surprised. He was sitting on the next stool, bounded on the south by Cynthia.

'What are you pair doing here?'

'Flexitime,' said Brannigan, referring to the enlightened work practices of the company.

'And who's minding the phone?'

'I left it off the hook,' Cynthia said, sipping politely at what I took to be a Scotch and red lemonade, her favourite morning drink.

'Anything in the post?'

'Just a Solicitors' letter looking for the rent.'

'Cheeky bastards.'

'We should wire an extension down here,' Brannigan suggested. 'Young Thady is good at that class of thing.' I gave myself a mental memo to look into that matter on a healthier day.

'And where were you going in the fancy motor car?' asked Brannigan who had evidently seen me dismount from the Papal limousine. Being reminded made me furious again.

'Wheeling round the town with a representative of Christ's Vicar on earth and being insulted and threatened out of my life, no less.' The more the gin warmed me the more furious I became.

'Desperate,' said Cynthia, tossing her head.

'Sitting there like Lord Muck,' I continued, 'casually throwing out insults and making threats as if he owned the bloody place.'

'That man should be kneecapped in the head,' said Brannigan earnestly. 'What did he say?'

'Said more or less that if we opened our mouths we'd be strangled — or probably suicided out the bloody window.'

'You wouldn't find Father Coddle saying that,' Cynthia remarked. 'He was a lovely man.'

'And then, if you don't mind; told me that I was a drunken fool and the only reason they picked me was that if I did open my mouth nobody would believe a blind bloody word of it.' A fury took me. 'I won't be insulted by some upstart witchdoctor from the Catholic Church!'

'But what exactly does he want us to do?'

'I still don't know, but the Church is at the back of it. We'll be told that in due course by the Nuncio, no less.'

'The slippery article up in the Park?' asked Brannigan.

'That's no way to speak about Mrs. Robinson,' Cynthia put in indignantly. I sighed, nodding to Brannigan.

'But he parted?' Brannigan said, like a man coming to the point.

I came to my senses. The cunning fellow had seen me pay for my round of three drinks for myself with a fifty pound note and off handedly wave Christy to keep the change; not that, with the price of drink in that establishment, that would have amounted to a munificent sum. Everything is watched, I noted sadly.

'Threw in a few miserable hundred for drinking money.'

'Desperate,' said Cynthia again. Brannigan was thoughtful, clearly coming to a different point of view.

'Well, bejasus, if a man is prepared to put up drinking money for the parched and underprivileged citizens of the nation, I, for one, am prepared to put up with all the insults and threats he can make.'

The more I drank, the more I saw that Brannigan, in his way, was a man who took the broad view. There was merit in what he said.

Chapter Three

Brannigan sat on the corner of his chair reading the paper. His wrists and knees were set at an angle of ninety degrees between which the paper spread like a great white wall. Brannigan could not read without reporting his reactions to anybody who cared to listen and from over the top of the wall issued a spasmodic stream of comments and ejaculations of the name of the second Divine person. 'Bollocks!' 'Stupid cunt!' 'Jasus!' 'Oh shit!' Reading the paper invariably worked him into a frenzy of indignation.

If there's one thing I detest, it's people who cannot register surprise or indignation without voicing expletives and coarse words. Surely to God, we can all express ourselves without using the argot of the party rooms or the soldier's billet. Everywhere you go now-a-days, there's nothing but bad fucking language at every hands turn. Nonetheless, I sympathised. I had long since given up reading any paper. Foreign news was inevitably reported from correspondents who were the crypto agents of British Intelligence or the C.I.A. and home news consisted mainly of what politicians were reported to have said — and only a cretin would believe a word of that — and what Fine Gael 'believes', sometimes spiced with the latest outcry against the availability of condoms by the Bishops; who appeared obsessed with nothing but sex — and damn the wife, chick or child between the lot of them. Social comment, if any, was usually the sniping of some bitch journalist against another, or fawning reports of the latest extravagances of the rip-off merchants or their fur clad and broad bottomed wives.

What passed for critical review of the arts was clearly written by illiterates who had spent the performance clinging to the theatre bar or read the book-flap while grunting on the lavatory. Every second captain of industry lionised by the press seemed to flourish for a time before spending some years in prison for making off with poor people's money. The only thing which took my serious attention was the Crossaire in the *Irish Times* at which I became so adept that I could no longer do the Simplex on a bad day. Brannigan, by contrast, who would neither eat his breakfast nor move his bowels without going through the paper from front to back, line by line, tended to believe most of what he read which gave him a very coloured view of reality. Cynthia's reading, while I am about it, was confined to the numbers on Lotto tickets or, in moments of acute boredom, going through the birth columns and laughing her brassier loose at the names with which some parents afflicted their unfortunate offspring. Nonetheless, listening to Brannigan's outbursts gave one a tentative idea of what might conceivably be going on.

'Jasus!' Like a man working against paralysis, he lowered the paper slowly and presented a stricken countenance to us. I am not a spoilsport. On cue, I obliged.

'What is it now?'

His jaw sagged to his chest, his eyes rolled like the white ball hopping round the Jackpot wheel and for some moments he affected to be made mute by visitation of God. It was a performance well worth the courtesy of our focussed attention.

'Oh, do tell us,' I pleaded in my best David Norris manner. He swallowed heavily and lowered his voice to a strangled gasp of incredulity.

'Delaney has got a medal from the Pope! Oh, sweet mother of divine Jesus!'

With a mighty bound, surprising in a man of my age, I was across the room and had wrenched the paper from him. I brought it to the window and read aloud avidly. It was true. That is, the report was there in the customary newsprint black and white. As my eye skidded across each line, I confirmed to myself that whatever uncertainties I might have had as to what day of the week it was, it was certainly not April the first.

'I don't believe it,' I gasped, quoting Adam on learning that the deity had demanded possession of the garden for the mere eating of a Granny Smith. But there it was. For dedicated service, quietly but loyally rendered, to S.P.U.C., the Knights and miscellaneous other right wing Catholic fronts sworn to the preservation of the national Hypocrisy, the Holy Father had been pleased to bestow on Hubert Xavier Delaney the Papal Order of Saint Stanislaus the Great and elevate him to the status of a Loved Son of Cosmos and Damien. A head and shoulders shot of Delaney depicted the boorish, platter-like face in the repose of smug righteousness, and a brief interview reported the Minister as giving his considered opinion that if one thing was more important than another, it was the stability of family life — a broad minded approach, I thought, from one known to maintain a stable of mistresses with more form than Arkle. Wild eyed, I gazed round the room for the plastic bucket which normally stood in the corner with an inch or two of Parazone in the bottom for spontaneous heavings on a seedy morning. The headline danced before me. POPE TO HONOUR GOVERNMENT MINISTER. A sickening reference was made to the exemplary standards of his Christian life.

'A Papal Count, no less,' echoed Cynthia chattily, casually filing her nails and not unduly aghast at the latest aberration of the Wily Pole.

'A Papal Cunt,' muttered Brannigan. I detest people who misuse that word but in the exigencies of the moment I was prepared to let it pass. As the shock ebbed, I fell to deep thinking. The usual scandals apart, Delaney's only public proclamations I could recall over recent years were his loud opposition to divorce and contraception and a gratuitous and cowardly insult to Mrs. Robinson which had secured her election as President of Ireland. His more usual public utterances took the form of stuttering and stammering his way through a prepared script written for him by some literary civil servant, articulating as best he could concepts far beyond his intellectual capacity. A typical television gaffe was his attribution of the conclusion 'I think, therefore I am' to an Irish poet he named as Des Carty.

'There's something afoot,' I said grimly, never the one to evade the obvious and organising my features into a thoughtful likeness to the late Mr. Sherlock Holmes.

'Desperate'.

'The hoors are up to something,' Brannigan agreed. 'Rome, like equity, does nothing in vain.'

But what? It was time for some detailed research as I had not been au fait with Church affairs.

'That's the handiwork of the sly article in the Park,' remarked Brannigan. That seemed a reasonable assumption; but what did I really know about these people?

In the days which followed I made no less than sixteen appointments which miscellaneous dentists, turned up half an hour too early and then scarpered from the premises before the screams of the patient before me died away to a broken sobbing. In the interval, I sat in their waiting rooms carefully reading through various back numbers of new magazines and *Sunday Times* supplements. I was also much indebted during my researches to the London publication, *Private Eye*, and by balancing the content of these issues with the more sugary outpourings of religious magazines, I was able to form some picture of recent Church politics. If quarter of what I read was to be believed, the Nuncio, Archbishop Luigi Castrato Cojones, was as sly an Italian diplomat as ever greased his way from the banks of the Tiber. He interfered constantly in political matters, summoned members of the Government to the Nunciature at will to give them their instructions and reported back to Rome like the head boy in a boarding school who wished to keep well in with the head master. Little else was known, apparently, of the oily Nuncio who kept a low public profile. I began to look forward to meeting him with all the curiosity of a visitor to the zoo viewing the reptile house for the first time.

I returned to the office one afternoon to find Brannigan on the phone.

'That's no problem to us,' he was saying. 'We'll ring the Department of Finance and ask that they be cleared without Customs examination. The precedent is there.'

Thady's Oklahoma accent sounded from the other end.

'Mild steel,' answered Brannigan.

Further difficulties from Thady. Brannigan again.

'Ah, for fuck's sake! Can't ye relabel the boxes? It's done here all the time. Listen, by the way; would ye not throw in a few Scud missiles for good will? The luck penny, like?'

Thady's tone seemed to indicate that that was easier said than done.

'Jasus,' replied Brannigan, 'ye're the mean pack of hoors and no mistake about it.' Cynthia began gesturing.

'Get off the bloody phone, will you,' she said. Brannigan brought his performance to an end in an avalanche of abuse.

'Jack, Monsignor Casserole was on for you.'

'What did he want?'

'Wouldn't say. Wouldn't leave a number. He'll ring you back.'

I looked at my watch.

'Well he better be quick about it. I want a drink.' I paced an uneasy round of the floor. 'Look, I'll be down below. Call me if he rings.' And at that moment the phone rang. Cynthia answered it as if she were Emer O'Kelly reading the news. She rolled her eyes heavenward and passed over the receiver.

'Doctor O'Toole,' I said.

'You will be collected at eight,' said a frozen voice. 'See that you are sober and properly turned out. The woman is to be demurely attired.' I glanced over at Cynthia. Despite a seasonal harshness of weather, she was wearing a skirt with a thigh slash cut well above the knee. If her blouse were cut any lower, her pubic hair would have been visible in minimal flying conditions to the skipper of a 747 on approach to Runway 24, five miles off the threshold. I could only guess her effect on a man suffering from celibate neurosis.

'Where are we going?' I asked bluntly. I did not like being told what to wear and I had already decided that tactics might be better served if Cynthia appeared as she was. The phone clicked dead in my ear.

'Ignorant bollocks!' I clapped my hands enthusiastically. 'We're up to the slippery fellow tonight.'

'Well, bejesus, we're not,' argued Brannigan. 'I'm taking the mother to Bingo.'

'I'm going out with Pauline,' Cynthia said. 'She's after finding two tickets in the loo for Frank Sinatra at the Point. I'm not missing that.' She extended her arms giddily. 'Fly me to the moon ... let me swing among the stars ....'

I looked scornfully at them.

'The Bingo will keep. As for Sinatra, if Sinead O'Connor gets a kick at him his next outing will be as the boy soprano in Babes in the Wood.'

'No way, Jack. I'm not putting the mother off again.'

'And I'm not going off to some convent up in the Park with Frank Sinatra live at the Point.' Letting it all hang loose, she began clicking her fingers in what purported to be a swinging rhythm. 'Come fly with me ... Come fly with me ... Let's fuck off somewhere and fuck ....'

I was quite shocked. Father Coddle's sad words about the Twelve came back to me. If there's one thing I can't stand it's the fickle friend; those who steal away in the hour of need.

'For God's sake. Are you telling me that you're going to back off just as the biggest deal we've ever had is coming to the boil?'

'I'm telling you that my mother is very important to me.'

'...... my ...... way.'

I am, whatever my little faults, a charitable man with

a compassionate understanding of the frailty of the human condition. Though the cynic will sneer, it is central to my belief system that there is in the core of all of us an innate goodness. Speak to that goodness and it will answer. I sat down heavily at my desk.

'Look, let me ask you both something.' I paused for effect, silently counting to three. 'Where exactly are you going? Just answer me that.'

'I'm going to Saint Anthony's Hall for Bingo,' Brannigan said uncompromisingly.

'I'll be at the Point Depot, Dublin One. '... And that's why this chick is a tramp ....'

I shook my head wearily.

'I didn't mean that. I didn't mean tonight. I meant in life. Where the hell are you going in life?'

'Wha'?'

'Don't mind him. He's going to come on all serious.'

'You're right. I'm asking you both a bloody serious question. Do you want to spend the rest of your lives as PAYE scrubbers having your pay packets ripped off to feed the fat cats? Is that what you want? Fuck off with ye so and play bingo and listen to that Mafia choirboy.'

Brannigan blinked. Cynthia didn't.

'Don't mind him,' she insisted. 'I know him. He'd talk the knickers off the Pope's wife.'

There was no more to be said. I stood up and made disdainfully for the door.

'Very well. No doubt you can afford to buy your own drinks.' I fumbled the door knob for long enough for Brannigan to react.

'Look, Jack, you're right. We'll have a good old talk in the morning.'

'I won't be in in tomorrow. If you want to ring me, I'll be staying at the Berkeley Court.'

'The Berkeley Court?' Brannigan laughed nervously. 'And how are you going to pay for that, may I ask?'

'By keeping my eye on the fucking ball!'

'Desperate,' said Cynthia.

Brannigan was weakening.

'Tell you what, Jack. We'll all go down and have a jar.

That's what we'll do. And you can tell us what's what. You're a sound bloody man, Jack O'Toole; fair play to you.'

'Alright so.' I turned to Cynthia. 'You can take yourself off to Old Blue Eyes.'

'Now wait a minute, Jack. There's no call to be so rude. You weren't so high and mighty this morning when you asked me to ....'

'... Oh, all right, Cynthia. You come too.'

We descended in unison, pari passu, seriatim, per stirpes, to the Fart and Arse and took our usual after hours position at the cosy end of the bar far from the draught at the street door. The premises was filling slowly with the common man slaking his thirst after a day of honest toil.

'Sorry, Jack,' Christy said. 'The slate is full.'

'Fear not, Doctor. There's wine from the royal Pope. The ships are in sight and by Angelus time tomorrow I shall personally discharge all liabilities, costs, claims, damages and demands con brio, tout de suite, quam celerimae, instanter and without let or hindrance, know ye all men by these presents, so help me God.'

'Does that mean yiz are going to pay?'

'Pressed down and overflowing.'

'Does that mean "yes"?'

'Yes.'

He backed away without taking his eyes off us, bequeathing to us a dubious and troubled look. I breathed a little easier when I saw him take the glasses from the shelf. I turned to Brannigan and ran my fingers down the lapel of his suit.

'It turned well. Where did you buy it?'

He paused for thought.

'Jasus, I have it so long now I don't remember.'

With equal condescension I pawed lightly at Cynthia's checkered jacket.

'Christian Dior, no doubt?'

'Ah, Jesus, isn't he a laugh a line? Zig and Zag isn't in it with you.'

'I thought as much. Sweated labour from Taiwan,

courtesy of Dunne's.'

She sneered angrily.

'Jesus, do you hear him? You're no tidy piece yourself, Jack, ould son. Jesus, Brannigan, the cheap suit of him and his zip got stuck and I had to pull it open for him and then, of course, he wanted ....'

'Alright, Cynthia, point made, very funny. But I'm trying to do something about it. It goes back to what I was saying. Where are you going in life?' I looked at each of them in turn. 'The Bingo Hall? The Point Depot?'

Neither dared to answer. I was beginning to command my audience.

With a tight expression of disapproval, Christy brought the tray and set the glasses in front of us. Here was no welcoming innkeeper, but a patronising and hard hearted man who despised the poor. The down trodden more than any others must keep up the brave front.

'A blessing on you, Christy. Now, like a good man, set up the same again. We will be disposing on the case at hearing very smartly.' He went off in a distinct sulk.

'Well,' Cynthia was saying, 'if I have to go up to the Park tonight, I'm going on afterwards to see Mrs. Robinson.'

I jeered.

'Are you joking? Did you think Nicholas would let you in the door and you dressed like a hoor on duty?'

Angry tears glistened in her eyes.

'Fuck you, Jack O'Toole. Mrs. Robinson said that anyone could come and see her. Smart arses like you can sneer all you like, but, at least Mrs. Robinson will have time for me.'

I realised slowly that she was serious. And what was more to the point was that if she did get as far as the hall door, without getting a blast from an Uzi, the President would very probably welcome her in. Mrs. Robinson was an imponderable enigma. A politician with integrity. A voice for the voiceless. I could never think about her without feeling like a mathematician trying to square a circle. But it didn't suit our necessity for deep cover if Cynthia was going to make herself a constant visitor at Aras an Uactarain. Unwelcome publicity might follow and that wouldn't do. It was Brannigan who relieved the dilemma.

'Ah, lissen, Cynthia, we'll go another time. Sure, she'd only be firing tea and biscuits into us and keeping us up all night with chat. We're too busy now. We've things to do.'

Cynthia bit her lip defiantly.

'It's Frank Sinatra or it's Mrs. Robinson. I'm not wasting me night with some jumped up Bishop.'

'Where are you going in life, Cynthia?' I intoned hypnotically. She looked at me, blinking her tears away.

'In this life, you can either screw or be screwed.'

'And that's for sure,' nodded Brannigan. I was coming to see that Brannigan was a man who prized the very real values.

'Look, Cynthia,' I continued, 'you can spend the rest of your life working for buttons and having your paypacket raped every week, like the thousands and thousands of others, scrimping and saving, pulling the devil by the tail, dining out on fish and chips, and buying your cigarettes in tens. And for what? So that your little pennies and the pennies of nurses, shop girls, guys working from six in the morning can be gathered together and handed over to the politicos and their pals for free booze, double pensions for doing nothing, and nineteen per cent pay increases. Do you think their mistresses are going around in recycled rags from Dunnes? Is your father still out of work?'

'Don't you say anything about my father.'

'I'm not. It wasn't his fault that the works went bust and he was fucked out after thirty years. It's not his fault that he's queuing up for a pittance. A politico would spend more on his lunch than your Da would collect in three weeks. Who pays your Da's bus fare when he's going down to sign on? A fat cat on a free junket to Brussels would be flown out in a Government Lear Jet. And do you know what they call the likes of your Da?'

'What?'

'A sponger.'

'Well, fuck them.'

'And do you know what they call the fat cats?'

'What?'

'Top people.'

She didn't answer.

'So when you get a chance to lay your hands on a bundle of money for doing a stroke for the Church or anybody else, you don't fool around. So that's why Frank Sinatra can go and fuck himself and any other waitress he can draw the knickers off. What sort of tickets have you got?'

'Down at the back,' she whispered.

'Where will the fat cats be sitting? And what are they using for money? The funds they've ripped off from some hospital ward that can't stay open while some old lady like Brannigan's Ma is breathing her last out in the corridor with some kid nurse looking after her and fifty others. And when the kid nurse gets her pay packet at the end of the week, the guts will be gone out of it to help pay for some unfrocked pig jobber who's wheeling round the town in a Government Mercedes. And the same fucker couldn't find his arse in the dark with both hands.Christy, for fuck sake, have you no compassion?'

Brannigan was suitably impressed by my political theories.

'You're right, Jack. Fuck Bingo.'

'Cynthia?'

'If they called me Da a sponger, I'll ....'

'You'll zero in on the main chance and make it work and then you'll have enough bred to fly Sinatra in to Dolphin's Barn to sing to you privately.'

Brannigan was shaking his head.

'Isn't it a wonder the Church doesn't speak out?'

'Why should it? The Church is ripping off public money too to fund the schools to brainwash the children. Once there's no sex involved, the Church doesn't give a shit. Why should they? The Bishops are top people too, don't forget.'

Cynthia was becoming dangerously furious.

'I'll fucking well tell Mrs. Robinson, so I will.'

'Mrs. Robinson knows. Don't worry. She'll take them out in her own good time. Now, fuck the begrudgers. We'll have the few scoops to put us in form for the druids.'

Christy was being a bit bolshie but there is good in all of us and even the most churlish of men will respond to a courteous approach which calls forth the best in him. Our little cares were well forgotten when a chilling breeze from the street door bowled down through the bar, caressed the legs of my trousers and rose within to fondle the hairs on my rectum with icy effect.

'Will someone close that fucking door!'

But a sinister presence stood framed therein. Tall and erect, Adolf Eichmann — I am certain it was he — booted and spurred, peaked cap to the eyes, arrogantly lifted his arm and clicked his fingers.

'We better finish these,' Brannigan said.

But there was no injury time allowed. Eichmann stamped his foot impatiently, beckoning.

'Desperate,' said Cynthia.

Chapter Four

If there's one thing I can't stand it's drunkenness. I can accept, indeed approve of, legitimate conviviality — in its proper place, of course — or the weary man who slakes his natural thirst after a hard day's work but against gluttony, alcoholic gluttony most of all, I draw an unflinching line. The very beasts of the fields will not so demean themselves. We were no sooner settled in the plush interior of the ecclesiastical limousine until Brannigan drowsed back in the cushions, his mouth gaping open in a disgusting display of bovine vulgarity, and to my utter dismay, his hand thoughtlessly fondling Cynthia's inside thigh and travelling relentlessly North. Cynthia too, the brazen hussy, sank sensuously back, opened her legs like the up and over door of a two car garage, and abandoned herself to an inebriated purring of carnal delight. It was more than my conscience would allow to sit idly by and remain silent.

'Brannigan, if you've no respect for yourself, at least have some for the girl. Cynthia, for Christ's sake! You're not here for a D and C.'

They struggled up, grumbling and blinking.

'The Third Reich is watching us in the mirror,' muttered Brannigan. Indeed he was. The darkened mirror was filled with a venomous eye and an old lady hobbling across the street was obliged to make a sudden spurt lest she found herself suddenly before the judgment seat of Christ. The loudest sound was the hissing of the tyres in the rain as we sped through the lighted metropolis, up the quays with an arrogant disregard for cross traffic and out through the Phoenix Park.

'This is where Mrs. Robinson lives,' said Cynthia, brightening up again and peering interestedly into the darkness. The headlamps cut a path off the main road, in through an imposing gateway and the car tore across a gravelled area and in round the back of the Residence. A mesh wire lamp, probably bought in a joblot from Stalag 17 after the War, illuminated the tradesman's entrance. We squeezed to a halt. Eichmann bounded out, opened the rear door and jerked his head.

'Get out.' A frigid figure awaited us in the doorway. It was Monsignor Casserole. His mouth fell open angrily as he glared at each of us in turn.

'You were instructed to be formally dressed.'

'Ah, fuck off,' growled Brannigan.

'What!?'

I simpered obsequiously, gathering myself with an effort.

'I am sorry, Monsignor. I had just asked him for the name of the Soviet Foreign Minister and he said "Molotov". We're always playing quiz games, you see. It keeps us sharp.'

I was wide awake now and determined to re-establish a grip on my straggling disciples. As the Monsignor led us down gloomy corridors beneath the supercilious gaze of the hanging portraits, I sizzled to them in a savage whisper.

'Keep your mouths shut from now on, both of you. Jesus, if either of you blow this, I'll be playing with your cards in the morning.'

His sensitive nose wrinkling in obvious disapproval, Casserole preceded us into a long, coffin shaped room. There was a heavy smell of wax polish and Church incense and at the top, a long table, braise covered in the Papal colours with three plush chairs on the far side. Ranged in front three plain wooden ones; the normal setting for a Court Martial. Along the walls the pompous features of past Pontiffs leered down upon us. Cynthia located mean minded Paul and stuck out her tongue, fortunately unseen by the Monsignor.

'You will speak when you are spoken to and not before. You will stand when His Excellency enters. Now sit down and remain in silence.'

With a last icy glare, he strode out, pulling the massive mahogany door behind him.

'That fellow is a bit of a bollocks, isn't he?' said Brannigan chattily.

'Desperate.'

I rallied my troops.

'For Christ's sake, smarten up. We're into the biggest deal of a lifetime. I'll do the talking. I want no smart assed back chat from the sidelines.' It was make or break now. They had had far more drink than was good for them and the curious thing was that I myself was not as nervous as I thought I should be. On the wall behind the inquisition table, the stricken figure of Christ hung on his cross. Given the nature of the institution, it seemed the ultimate blasphemy. I straightened my tie and reviewed the others again.

'Cynthia, for fuck's sake will you pull down your skirt. You're not above in Dolly Fawsitt's now. Brannigan, sit up.'

The door at the top opened with a crack and three churchmen filed in. An odd canonical assortment. First came Casserole, half turned and looking behind him, then the Nuncio himself, Archbishop Cojones and a younger priest who took my eye immediately. He was a prototype, short back and sides Opus Dei product, in formal black soutane and an old fashioned hard Roman collar. Icy as holy water, I thought, his coldness perceptible across the room. I studied him. The resemblance to that obedient patriot, Colonel Oliver North was arresting and I could well visualise him dispassionately strangling Signor Calvi while devoutly murmuring, 'All for Jesus, through Mary.' Without realising it, we had come to attention and so remained until the triumvirate seated themselves in front of us. Dismissively, Casserole waved to us to sit.

With the exception of a dwarf in the pay of Duffy's

Circus, the Papal Nuncio was the smallest man I had ever seen in my life. In his flowing crimson robes he looked like Queen Victoria in drag or a pet monkey on new, extra, family sized stilts. He had a tiny monkey's face with a pair of incredibly bright brown eyes which scanned us disinterestedly and then lifted themselves to some indeterminate point over our heads. So, this, I thought, was the most powerful man in Ireland. It was to this diminutive cleric, unelected by anybody, that the Government, elected by the people who paid them well, touched the forelock, begging permission before legislating for any social progress. His voice, when he spoke, was small and squeaky, his English fluent and only slightly accented.

'Our Holy Father,' he began without preamble, 'is heavy hearted and sorrowing. He knows no peace.'

'That's good news,' murmured Brannigan down his chest. I cleared my throat ostentatiously and angled myself in my chair to shatter his shin bone if he as much as opened his mouth for a breath of air for the remainder of the evening.

'Some years ago, with a heart flowing with love, his very soul aflame he came amongst his cherished Irish children and enjoined upon them certain things. Though wearied from travelling, he went tirelessly amongst your people, patiently expounding the way of truth and light.' With sudden anger, the brown eyes flashed. 'The Holy Father knows exactly what he said!'

'How do you mean he knows exactly what he said?' Brannigan interrupted. 'Sure, the man is hardly astray in the head.' He was quite drunk and his voice had the irritated tone of one who hadn't much time for bloody nonsense. But enough was enough. With a merciless swing, I sank the toe of my shoe into the marrow of his bone. I was rewarded at once with a whimper of suppressed agony and saw the tears spurt from his eyes. Up at the table, the Nuncio stopped abruptly, glanced from one acolyte to the other and frowned. Monsignor Casserole bent towards him and a whispered consultation ensued. Colonel Oliver North looked on anxiously.

After some moments of discussion, they drew apart and Casserole spoke.

'You will understand that the Holy Father is not fluent in the English tongue. While he was here amongst you, his speeches were composed for him by the Irish Hierarchy and read phonetically. His Excellency makes the point that even though that situation obtained at the time, His Holiness was later briefed on his Irish visit and is now fully conversant with what he said and the strictures he laid down at that time. Now, you will kindly not interrupt His Excellency again and any questions you may have will be addressed to me afterwards.' He turned and nodded respectfully to Archbishop Cojones.

'Mind you,' grunted Brannigan between sobs, 'I can remember him pleading on his bended knees and he standing bolt upright.' He remained bent double and rubbing his shin. I dangled my toe menacingly under his nose.

The Nuncio whined on. It appeared that the Wily Pole had been increasingly distressed ever since to find that his words had fallen on heedless ears. His Holiness's ardent and deeply treasured belief that Ireland was the last truly Catholic State, a belief which had sustained him through many arduous years, was crumbling in ashes. Every report from Ireland brought fresh and disturbing news of increasing decadence. Apart from political violence about which the Holy Father could be philosophical, given the part it had played in the Church's rise to power, and worsening economic conditions, poverty and unemployment which were, of course, the will of God and no more — what, fie, of other matters? Despite the clear ruling of the Church, overt advocacy of divorce and contraception was now becoming the norm! These views were being openly expressed! Gravely sinful matters were being spoken of as 'rights'!

As he proceeded, His Excellency appeared to have increasing difficulty in concentrating. Time and again, he lost the flow of his eloquence and his eyes strayed repeatedly to where Cynthia was sitting, his squeaking voice trailing away into a distracted silence. Perplexed, I glanced towards Cynthia. What I saw put me to the verge of cardiac arrest.

She was sitting back in her chair, legs crossed and the ankle swinging, with an economic holding of silken thigh casually exposed. While her face was showing every sign of polite boredom, her tongue was flicking provocatively along her lips and her eyes were resting speculatively upon Colonel Oliver North. The frigid priest was returning her gaze with an unmasked hatred. Then, quite suddenly, Casserole took a hand in the proceedings. He clicked his fingers.

'The woman will sit at the back of the room,' he ordered. I had had a little too much of these peremptory commands. We were entitled, God knows, to some respect from this coven of warlocks.

'Now, just a goddam minute, if you please ....'

Immediately, Monsignor Casserole switched his glare to me.

'Mr. O'Toole, are you interested in this assignment or not?'

First things first, of course.

'Hey, Cynthia, like a good girl, go down and sit at the back. There's a good girl.'

'Aren't they the randy bag of fuckers just the same?' muttered Brannigan, with some grudging admiration. As Cynthia tripped unconcernedly down the room the Nuncio paused, brought his joined hands to his lips in prayer, coughed delicately and resumed.

'Sexual intercourse, once properly regarded as a regrettable matrimonial duty, is now treated as some kind of therapy! A matter of sport and levity!' With these words, the papal fury burst upon us. Quivering with rage, the little Nuncio began to shout. Worse was happening, worse, worse, worse! A distinct campaign was in train for the enhancement of the status of women! People were talking about women's 'rights!' 'Rights!' no less! Nobody had rights once the Church had spoken! Clinics had been opened for sterilisation, for rape crisis counselling, for battered wives! Trendy liberalism was all! It was bad enough that attendances at weekly Mass were falling, but if half what the Holy Father had heard was true, every second person in prominent public positions was maintaining a mistress to the common knowledge of all the simple faithful! Despite all his injunctions to the contrary, lustful men were trading in obsolete wives for newer models and this practice had become widespread! Unmarried mothers, instead of being flogged from their villages, were being paid! The word 'paid' rose in a scream which hopped off the oak beamed ceiling. With all the manipulative skill of a Redemptorist giving a Retreat, the Nuncio dropped his voice to a regretful whisper. While the Holy Father could always understand and be compassionate of human fraility, the on-going state of affairs in the country was, if His Excellency might employ a figure of speech which he understood to be in the Irish idiom, 'tearing the arse out of it altogether.'

Casserole fixed us with a lethal look which clearly betokened immediate strangulation by Colonel Oliver North if we dared to even smile, and he drew hurriedly on the Nuncio's sleeve. Once again the three heads joined in fraternal conclave, a buzz of urgent whispering broke out and the Monsignor seemed to be explaining something very complicated. The Nuncio's face took on a very grave look and the purselike mouth hardened into a strict, self disciplining line. Resolutely, he faced to us again.

'I am advised that my command of the local idiom is unfortunate and I humbly beg the forgiveness of my Father in heaven and of you, my brothers and, eh, my, eh, ... sister.' He paused again, recollecting himself and presumably gave himself to moments of penitential prayer. Then he continued.

'Immediate steps have been ordered by the Holy Father for the reconversion of Ireland. The time for tolerance, delay, speculation, prolonged planning, social research has passed. Immediate action is the watchword. A dramatic, drastic initiative is called for. No expense will be spared, no effort is to be restrained.' The

Nuncio's voice narrowed to a low, cold, deliberation. He eyed us significantly. 'In carrying forward the Gospel of Jesus Christ, the Church's message to the Irish people, no method is to be ruled out. Effectiveness is everything!' The Nuncio allowed a portentous silence fill the room. His eyes remained riveted to ours. Then, his voice breaking with emotion, he spoke again.

'No piteous words of mine can express the aching, burning love which the Holy Father feels for your people. Night and day, his heart is tortured by his pure, unutterable love ....'

My eyes wandered to Brannigan's face. The cynical amusement I felt myself but was astute enough to conceal was openly playing across his flushed, inebriated countenance. He had the unmistakable appearance of an affable drunk who was thoroughly enjoying a subtle but professionally rendered comedy turn. As the possibility that he would burst out laughing or, worse still, inaugurate a round of applause in which Cynthia would surely join, grew greater, I felt the hair stand out on the back of my neck. I set myself fair for a further punitive kick at his shins and by way of warning began to swing my ankle carelessly beneath his gaze so that the warning would not go unheeded. If he ended the night in the Blackrock Clinic, he would only have himself to thank for that expensive misfortune. And yet I could sympathise. I had always marvelled at the way these people could prostitute language. A ruthless totalitarian state will style itself as a 'People's Democratic Republic'. A politician will speak movingly of his 'integrity' and the 'high standards' to which he adheres in public life. A blonde bitch with forty fur coats will proclaim herself the 'Champion of the Shirtless Ones'. A seedy Italian bank which laundered forged bonds for the Mafia will trade as 'The Institute for Religious Works'. An international conspiracy to condition with voodoo the minds of the masses will refer to itself as 'Holy Mother' and as it employs the subtlest techniques of fear, guilt and remorse for manipulation and conditioning, proclaim itself to be 'the Pillar and Ground of Truth'. Not entirely by coincidence my eyes strayed along the wall and rested upon the mean, tight mouthed, piercing eyed portrait of the mean and miserable Paul who had crucified the lives and marriages of millions before people learned to think for themselves. And this was the institution whose normal parlance was fruity with references to 'love', 'compassion' and 'caring'. Very quickly, my sardonic amusement began to turn to a whitehot fury and it was only the prospect of acquiring vast quantities of coin of the realm which kept me from jumping to my feet, striding out, and slamming the door with enough vengeance to splinter the panelled cabinet-work from the hinges. Trembling with rage, I jerked my eyes to the next portrait and felt my heart skip like a child's kite soaring on a high wind into the sun.

For one moment, the radiance of Good Pope John seemed to flood into the room. I felt my eyes moisten and my mind spiral into an extraordinary spiritual speculation. Could it be that Christ had come again in the person of this loving, fatherly man who had reached fearlessly to embrace the whole world, denying himself to none. I had been a schoolboy then, but precociously conscious of the evils of Catholicism. Suddenly I was back again, joyous with the hope that this beautiful man would lead the Church, screaming and kicking, onwards to Christianity. Love wouldn't be a dowdy, four letter word any more, but a real, vibrant way of living. What can I do for you? would be the cry. Let me do something for you — for the hell, the high and the kick of it. Hell, no thanks. I don't want anything back. I glimpsed in myself a sudden and strange realisation. If that smiling man was Pope still, Jack O'Toole would be kicking down the doors of the Churches to get into first Mass every morning of his life. Then the dream vanished and I was back with my ears tuning again to the Nuncio's squeaks, and Christ himself was no more than a Jungian archetype, a king in Camelot; gone like Mother Goose and Santy Claus and those other innocent deities of childhood. Brannigan was beginning to blubber with glee.

'Brannigan,' I pleaded in a whisper, 'for Christ's sake,

think of your mother.' I twisted in my chair and shot a furtive glance back at Cynthia. In the relative gloom at the back of the room, she was nodding off, her legs spread apart like the main gate at Dublin Castle and her high heels dug into the carpet to brace herself. May all the Saints of heaven, the Little Flower and the Big Flower, grant and vouchsafe that she would not slide on to the floor and curl up in her sleep. But the Nuncio's voice had taken a cunning, scheming tone.

'But be that as it may, Mrs. Robinson is an interesting phenomenon. While she may have abused the legal processes — and often without reward, I understand — in pursuit of what these people dare to call "rights" and paid scant attention to the words of our Holy Father, she is greatly loved by the people.' His little mouth worked silently for a moment. 'I find that interesting. Very interesting. Significant. The message has not been lost upon us. What is plainly required at this moment of history is the shining example of a woman. A woman who will command the love and respect of common man.'

I had been experiencing some difficulty in staying awake and not a little resentment at being kept captive at what was essentially a Church sermon but I had to concede that I found the Nuncio's last words a most compelling observation. If President Robinson wouldn't do — though no matter what the cost I would have no truck with any effort to dislodge her from office — I did wonder who could be whistled in alongside to command the attention of the Irish people. Names fluttered through my mind. There was Twink, Nell McCafferty, Ann Doyle and maybe, fair play, Maeve Binchy. A writer? What about Patricia Scanlan, hell of a nice girl and well able to tell a good yarn if it came to that. While Bibi Baskin and her coupla focal used to send me screaming to the lavatory, there was no point in allowing prejudice prevail and the girl was just as much entitled to be considered as anybody else. What about Marian Finucane? Now there was a girl who would make people sit up and take notice. Clap a wig on Sinead O'Connor and who knows? Daniel O'Donnell was out, of course, but he could be brought along to pass the tea and seedy cake to the old ladies. A singer, perhaps? Madonna? In the second following, I knew that that had been a freudian slip for as the words of the Nuncio reached me again I felt my scalp tingle and my back straighten against my chair.

'We will invoke the presence of Mary, the Blessed Mother of God, the divine mediator at the feet of Christ.'

I gasped. I couldn't believe what I was hearing. After all my years of writing off the Christian hypothesis as an archetype mythology, a rag bag of superstition, could it be that there was in fact such a person as Mary? Childhood fears possessed me again. After all my contempt for these priests and everything they represented, could it possibly be that they had in fact strange powers and could invoke Mary — if she existed — to walk the earth again? An eerie uneasiness took me and a slippery sweat began to dampen my back. Near to terror, I began to concentrate on what the Nuncio was saying.

'Mary will crush the serpent under her heel!' He was shouting again. 'She will direct the Irish people! Her message will be heard and obeyed! Tower of David!'

Even Brannigan was impressed.

'Star of the Sea,' he roared back before I could stop him. I compressed his elbow in a vicegrip of steel.

'Star of stage, screen and radio,' piped Cynthia from the back who had unfortunately woken up.

'Order,' snarled Casserole, searing us with his eyes. The Nuncio came to his feet without warning. His eyes bored into mine.

'There is no more to be said. Mr. O'Toole, you will arrange forthwith a spectacular and convincing apparition which will convey to the people in unmistakable terms the injunctions of the Holy Father. The petty details may be discussed with Monsignor Casserole.' He paused, his brown monkey eyes penetrating mine until they hurt. 'Father Luciano here will deal with any breaches of security.' With animal disinterest, the eyes with that mindless hatred of caged primates, Colonel North stared at me and for a horrific moment I had the sensation of being escorted from Liberty Hall via the top floor. Then, without farewell, the Nuncio turned and left the room, his reverend henchmen following respectfully in his flowing wake.

Brannigan was blinking and shaking his head.

'What the fuck was that all about?' he asked like a Dail Deputy waking up after a debate.

I began to wonder myself. I was less than a hundred per cent certain that I had heard what I had heard. Cynthia came dreamily forward, sucking her finger.

'I'm after breaking me nail,' she said. 'Jesus, isn't the little fellow a gas turn altogether? God be good to poor Mickser Reid. I enjoyed it, so I did.'

'Did you hear what he said?' I asked her.

'He was saying about Mrs. Robinson.'

'Brannigan, did you hear the bit about the Blessed Virgin?'

'Sort of. He seems to think she's coming back or something.'

I can't stand people who won't pay attention and get the message right. I'm sick to death of people messing and catfarting about and not listening.

'He bloody well seems to think that we're going to bring her back. That's what he seems to think.'

Brannigan nodded coolly.

'Yeah, that's what I thought. I wasn't sure, though.'

'And how in the name of fuck are we going to organise that, if you don't mind me putting an awkward question?'

He shrugged jauntily.

'Sure, what trouble is in it? Didn't the boyos do it years ago below in Knock and they having nothing but a magic lantern?'

Like a wafting ghost, Monsignor Casserole reappeared through the door and sat down in the central chair recently vacated by the Archbishop. Obediently, we sat down again. I was sobering fully with commendable alacrity.

'You are clear on your instructions?'

We weren't. In fact, I was never less certain in my life

that the drink hadn't brought me low at last and I wasn't in the grip of advanced delirium.

'Do you mind if I ask a question?' I opened. He nodded coldly and stared at me.

'Did I hear him say that the Blessed Virgin Mary is going to appear in Ireland?'

'Yes.'

'And we're supposed to rig some stunt to make that happen?'

'His Grace said no such thing. He said that you were to arrange a convincing and spectacular apparition.'

'A stunt, in other words?'

'His Grace didn't say that. He enjoined you to arrange it. How you do your business is none of ours and His Grace certainly gave no indication of that.'

I was becoming increasingly mystified. Casserole was constantly missing the delicate nuances of the point.

'Does he mean that we're to say prayers and light candles and sing hymns. Is it that sort of thing he means?'

The Monsignor's mouth curled at the corner.

'I beg leave to doubt that your prayers would be efficacious.'

I nodded.

'So it's a stunt he wants?'

'I wish you would desist from that gross slander. His Grace said no such thing but left the modus operandi entirely up to you.'

'The wha'?' asked Brannigan.

'The stunt,' I said. 'Listen, your Amazing Grace, the only way I can see it being done is a stunt — that's if we can do it at all.'

'That's your affair.'

'I see.' Problems and possibilities swirled in my mind. I said a little prayer to the soul of Blessed Sam Goldwyn. That seemed to free my thinking a little.

'We'd want a hell of a budget. This is a mega production we're looking at. As Sam said, we'd want to start with an earthquake and work up to a climax. We'll have to fly in Meryl Streep to play the part.'

'No,' he shouted, his face flooding. 'No. You are not to involve anybody else. That's an order.' His voice fell to arctic temperature again. 'Remember Signor Calvi, I enjoin you.'

The tension in the room would have squeezed millions for the Third World from the Department of Foreign Affairs and it was Brannigan who broke it by discharging a well chosen fart which reverberated hollowly against the four walls. If there's one thing which I can't stand, it's crass vulgarity but both the Monsignor and I, people who knew how to behave, ignored the pistol-like report unblinkingly.

'The woman looks Jewish,' the Monsignor remarked.

'What woman?' asked Cynthia, looking about her. Then I saw the anger ignite on her face. I froze her with a look.

'She's from Dolphin's Barn as it happens,' I said. 'Maybe with a bit of coaching ... couldn't we get Maureen Potter at the right price to teach her ....'

The Monsignor's fist came down on the table like the blow of a sledge hammer.

'I've already said that no one else is to be involved. You seem totally unable to assimilate the simplest instruction. Pull yourself together, if you please! Surely she has some experience of school plays.'

'Oh, yeah. She used to be pretty big in the R and R — that's the Ranelagh and Rialto Musical Society. Surely your grace has heard of the R and R?'

He nodded curtly.

'What was her stage name?'

'Shirley MacLaine,' put in Brannigan, now carelessly hazarding his privates against a kick from me.

'Junior,' I added hastily, for the man hadn't spent his life on the moon. 'Can we discuss all this with Father Coddle?'

'Father Coddle knows nothing. It will remain so.'

'What about Adolf, eh, your driver?'

'He knows nothing.'

'I see. So the Nuncio and the priest are the only ones?'

'His Excellency has expressed a wish and no more. As

loyal Catholics, that wish will be your command. Father Luciano heard that wish expressed and no more.'

'So, there's only yourself. Is that it?'

'I have listened to your idle chatter with patience. I know nothing else and I don't wish to. Now, unless there is anything else, you will depart about your business and we will wait prayerfully for the manifestation which His Excellency deems so urgently necessary.'

'So it's up to us to engineer the stunt.'

'That is for you. I am not concerned with the sordid workings of the public relations industry. The Holy Father's ordinances on current social matters are plain and I would suggest that you call at Veritas House and read closely of Lourdes and Fatima and familiarise yourself with the usual procedures in these matters. You will not make contact here again. Is that understood?'

'Yes, Your Principality. Now, like, em, what about the money? The outlay on a show like this will be enormous.'

'The driver will put you in funds. Funds are unlimited. You will be generously provided for at all times.'

A little smidgin of doubt troubled me. It would be better to clear the matter there and then.

'Lookit, Father, suppose, just suppose, like, that after all the money and after we trying our level best, shoulder to the wheel and all that; we just couldn't bring it off? What then, like?'

He gave me a calm, icy look. For a moment he seemed to be both weighing me and at the same time considering the moral dilemma which I had proposed for his guidance.

'That would be a matter of conscience, wouldn't it?'

That struck me as being a very reasonable approach. For all his sinister and forbidding ways, there was another side to him. Get him in a pastoral frame of mind and he wasn't half as bad as he seemed.

'That's what I was thinking myself,' I replied happily.

'A matter for the Confessional.'

'Exactly, Monsignor.'

'But then,' he went on silkily, 'you couldn't confess the sin without breaking the essential seal of secrecy.'

He was a man of amazing insight.

'Isn't that the good one, now. I never thought of that.'

'You would need a very discreet Confessor, wouldn't you?'

'Father Coddle,' I plumped at once. His face darkened again.

'No, Mr. O'Toole. No. Father Luciano. He is a caring and understanding man, zealous in his pursuit of souls. He would not alone confess you but administer the Last Rites. You would go to meet your Maker without the slightest stain of sin on your soul.' He rose calmly and left the room, his place taken at once by Adolf Eichmann. The warm, cloying, damp sensation of unpremeditated piss drew my trousers close to my leg and I followed Eichmann out with the others like Charles J. Haughey, Esq., T.D., performing his celebrated walking without breaking eggs routine. The smell in the car would mind an orchard.

Chapter Five

I am an easy going, broadminded, live and let live, what-are-you-having, sort of fellow; but if there's one thing that drives me to mania, it's slovenly people going around who won't keep themselves clean and tidy. No polish on the shoes, no proper shave and the suits on the half of them looking as if they slept in them. Then you have the hairy hussar brigade. Bushy growths being carefully cultivated on the upper lip and it growing wild on their arseholes. Little pony tails sticking out behind like Moby Dick — was he the whale or the whaler? — and damn the comb, apparently, between the lot of them. Surely to God, it's not too much to ask that a man will rub his shoes up the back of his trouser leg before he goes out or go down to the Burlington and steal a bar of soap and a bit of a towel and keep himself clean? God nose we owe it to the country and the people around us, if not to ourselves. But no. Mention the matter at all, the gentlest hint of a hint, and all you get back is the whinging, self-pitying complaint that they can't afford anything better; and the same people will be found night after night pouring drink after drink down their gluttonous gullets and then out like a greyhound from the trap, down the lane with them and up with the lot against the gable wall; beige cascades of projectile puke all slimy and green and bits of tomato and ham sandwiches floating in amongst the bubbles — the trousers ruined. I'll tell you one thing. It's not good enough.

The sun had hardly framed itself between the Pigeon

House chimneys that morning until down Grafton Street I went and turned in on the door of a Gentleman's Outfitter and Tailor.

'Three lightweight suits, please; six silk shirts, some discreet knitted ties, underwear and shoes.' The mousey little man behind the counter bent forward solicitously, beamed happily and washed his hands, for all the world like Pontius Pilate or the Minister for Justice who knew nothing about the heavy gang.

'Certainly, sir. Step this way, please.'

I've no time for those who fire money about as if they had been retailing Planning Permissions or Passports at the right price, but I had a position to think of. I was President and Managing Director of Image and Erections (International) Limited. I.E.I. was now a trans-European corporation, a keenly pitched, low intensity operation which would only deal with the best, blue chip clients — and none of your fly-by-night Insurance brokers, up-start authors, or politicians on the make and paying the fees from public funds.

Up to the Shelbourne for a haircut, a shave and a face massage. Then upstairs to the foyer and into the telephone booth. Long session. Identical calls to the Westbury, the Burlington, Jurys and the Berkeley Court.

'Will you page Doctor Jack O'Toole, please. You may announce that it is extremely urgent and that Washington is on the line.' It was a time to become known round the town.

I rang the office. Cynthia answered, giggling happily, Brannigan guffawing in the background. I frowned. I had noticed one or two things in recent days which were disquieting but I had kept my counsel. I am tolerant of the playful, teasing frolics of man and maid, for boys will be boys and girls will be girls, but if there's one thing I'm death on, and that's any hint of lewdness or loose behaviour. We are, God help us all, supposed to be rational, thinking beings and not instinctual brute animals.

'What the hell is going on over there?'

'Nothing, Jack, honesty. Are you coming in?'

If she hadn't said 'honestly' my mind would have been at rest but there had been an unsavoury note to her glee. I had a good mind to pretend to be going elsewhere and then steal up the stairs and catch them in flagrante; the pair of them spreadeagled on my desk and Brannigan's pimpled bum rising and falling like a carpenter's elbow and he at the sawing of a plank of plain deal.

'I shall be over later on. Anyone ring?'

'No.'

'Anything on the post?'

'Only a form. What? Sorry, just a minute, Jack. Yes. Brannigan says it's a Notice to Quit.'

'Quit what?'

'It's the office, Jack. It's about the rent. They want us out.'

I was furious. If there's one thing I can't stand it's upstart hop-me-thumbs who don't know their place. The Landlord was a greasy little ferret in a raincoat who seemed to own half Dublin but wouldn't fart a fugue to make music for the lonely.

'Well, fuck them. Didn't we pay them last month? What more do they want?'

'No point in shouting at me, Jack. I'm only working here.'

I had my doubts about that too, but after all the phone calls, my throat was gone as dry as Just a Thought on R.T.E. radio and I ambled into the Horseshoe Bar for medicinal purposes. The attendance was sparse and but for two blazered brigadiers with scarlet, beefy faces like bewhiskered bulldogs, escorted by a brace of vicious-faced old ladies in tweeds at the sherry and the usual coterie of suave business types in their pinstripes, their flat, black briefcases round their ankles; the bar was empty — or so I thought. But God knows, it's a gas bloody country just the same. Is it any wonder we're half bolloxed and bankrupt and half the bloody town out on the piss at eleven o'clock in the day instead of minding their business? A different calibre of man, I stood apart and summoned the barman.

'Double gin and tonic, my good man, slice of lemon,

tall glass.'

I had an inordinate shake in my hand thanks to my encounter with the One Holy Catholic and Apostolic Church the night before and I knew from experience that any effort to drink with finger and thumb on the stem of the more usual glass would shoot the nourishment up my sleeve and down my front, and with silk shirts coming at £120 a slice, a man must be circumspect in his ways.

'Bit of ice, sir?'

Will somebody explain to me what is the point in prosecuting publicans for diluting drink in the bottle and then permitting them to dilute it in the glass?

'No thank you.'

I gave my wrist a brisk rub and flexed my fingers. I then applied the law of reverse intent, and with all the cunning of an abattoir rat, rushed the glass when it wasn't looking and got the best of it down, damn the drop wasted. The hand steadied and I bade the barman to have the next case in the list ready for hearing, for the one before the Court would be settled at any moment. Then I saw her. Cole Porter's lyric: Is it an earthquake or is it a shock? sang through my mind, orchestration by Count Basie, arrangement by Nelson Riddle; Quincy Jones on standby. She was a long-legged American girl, blonde hair bouncing to her shoulders and swaying like a wheatfield in July, her arms and shoulders bare and bronzed. I'm not one of these gobshites whose jaw hangs open at anything foreign. For feeding hens, baking soda bread and wearing her womb to a tissue making souls for Christ, the Irish woman gives best to none and you'll get the odd one who hasn't been emotionally crippled by the nuns, who knows what's what when the lights go low as Jack O'Toole can personally and gratefully attest, but when winter beckons and the spirits sink; for stopping traffic, obstructing breath and putting one on a snowman, you'll travel many the mile before you'll do better than a virgin from Vermont or a maiden from Milwaukee. I couldn't take my eyes off her, wonderstruck that I hadn't noticed her, two stools upwind. With no permission from me, my head nodded in the friendly way of my race. I knew a moment of misgiving. She would either nod cooly or archly enquire if I was waiting for my wife. I was stunningly in error. The dazzling blue eyes warmed like the sun coming up on a lakeshore, a beatific smile broke across the whitest teeth I had ever seen and she stretched out her hand immediately.

'Well, hi there! I'm Vi Langley.'

I practically gaped as I took her hand and felt the long cool fingers touch mine.

'Hi. I'm Jack O'Toole.'

'Hiya, Jack. What do you do, Jack?'

I swallowed. The pace of the conversation would create wake turbulence but then Americans are like that. This lassie probably drove a Mustang on the fast lane all her life.

'I'm in public relations. I have a company here in town.'

'Well, hey now. Now ain't that something else? Gee, I love public relations.'

I tried to keep pace on the fast lane.

'Yeah, we do alright. What do you do yourself, Vi?'

'I'm head of the Mafia in Cincinnati.'

'You must do alright too ... sorry, say that again?'

'The Family. Cincinnati.'

'You said the Mafia?'

'Right.'

I drank deeply. One of these days I'm going to hear that the Pope has legged it to Rimini with Sophia Loren and when that day dawns I'm going to drink deeply too.

'Isn't, well, em — isn't that an unusual job for a woman?'

'Ah, come on Jack. You don't look like a M.C.P. to me.'

'Oh, I'm not, believe me. What's Cincinnati like?'

'Oh, you know. Like, industrial, I guess. It's a port on the Ohio river. Like maybe three fifty, four hundred thousand people, I guess. I don't live there, though. I live at Falls Church, Virginia.'

'Cowboy country?'

'Well, not quite. Suburb of Washington D.C.'

'Got you.' I drank deeply again. 'Look, do you mind if I ask you a question?'

'Shoot.'

'Did I hear you say you were head of the Mafia?'

'Right.'

'Well, isn't that a criminal organisation? At least that's what everybody in this country thinks.'

'It's a business, Jack, strictly business. But you gotta protect the investment.'

'But what about the drugs and the prostitution and all that?'

'Supply and demand, I guess. You do business and make money or somebody else will.'

'But what about people being bumped off? Hit men and all that sort of thing?'

She laughed openly.

'Oh, Jack, what kind of people do you think we are? That all went out with the round table at the Algonquin.' She shook her head, still smiling. 'No, no, no. You make it look like an accident.'

Ninety per cent of the gin went down the wrong way. When sound had been resumed, I thought I'd try her with another question. She seemed remarkably candid.

'But you still put out contracts on a guy?'

She sighed a beautiful sigh and shrugged.

'You ever hear of the C.I.A., the S.A.S., the K.G.B.? Mossad? Legitimate Government protecting their interests? What's the difference? Not very nice, I agree; but necessary.'

'Yeah, but look; let me ask you something else. You're a lovely person, Vi, but what if some other comedian gets ideas and takes one out on you?'

She smiled and reached over, resting a kindly hand on mine.

'Jack, you're sweet, you really are; and thank you for the "lovely person", but we're business people. We're civilised. I got soldiers on the streets.'

'Yeah. Of course. I never thought of that.'

She slipped sylphlike from the stool and moved right

up beside me, her knees tantalisingly touching mine. The Private Member, for some time stirring with curiosity, came out of his kennel on status one alert. Her eyes melted into mine like luscious laser beams. Various possibilities, not for viewing before eight o'clock at night, began to flicker across the widescreen of my imagination. I could only assume that the Almighty was smiling upon me at last, as a reward for the attentive hearing I had given to the representatives of the One True Church the night before. Nothing else could account for the breathtaking surge in my fortunes. Oh, how our standards change! There was a time when a grope in Mount Merrion woods would have warmed me for a week.

'Now, you. Tell me about your operation.'

Oh, no, I thought. How could I keep face if she discovered that I operated a little less expansively than was usual along Fifth Avenue? The agony of being unable to boast that my one client was probably one of the biggest in the world was oppressive but whatever the temptation, I had no intention of being fucked out the window of the Dart between Booterstown and Merrion Gates by the sinister Father Luciano as he raised his hand in the last absolution of my sins.

'Ah, it's pretty small, Vi. Nothing like New York. Nothing like anything you'd know about.'

'Discreet?'

'Would you believe that in the whole outfit, only three people know who each other is?'

'My. Now, that's what I call deep cover.'

'Yeah. I don't talk about it.'

'Hey now. Now you're making me homesick.'

'You here on business?'

'Naw. Just a little vacation. It's been a tough year.'

'You can say that again.'

'It's been a tough year.' She laughed gaily, her head falling forward, her lips achingly close to mine. She straightened up, her face becoming serious.

'Jack. Maybe we could do a little business some time?'

'You mean ....?' She laughed again.

'Jack, I could sue you for what's going through your mind. No, business.' She rubbed her finger and thumb together. 'Business, Jack. Covert operations, call it.'

'Yeah, that would be O.K.,' I said casually. I didn't really fancy the chance of standing in the dark and shooting some poor bugger through his bedroom window, and he standing in his braces wondering if his wife had taken her temperature; but if there was a few bob on hand for running a few innocent little messages I didn't mind tangling with the Mafia. There were a lot of people who didn't mind joining Fine Gael or Fianna Fail, or, indeed, if it came to that, Pancho's lot; or sliding silently through the Knights and having sold my soul to Archbishop Cojones and his masters, I was in no moral position to profess lofty, holier than thou standards.

'Right on, daddio. Let's talk about that sometime too. Hey, I like your suit.'

'Oh, this? Yeah, I fly them in from Paris.'

'Saint Germaine?'

'Saint Bernard.'

'Cute. Hey! Well, ringa-ding-ding! There goes Hughie. Hughie! Hughie! Come to Momma, boy!'

As Hughie Delaney turned and saw her, his bull like face broke into a sweaty grin. Knuckles almost brushing the carpet, he came over. Down deep into the hand stitched recesses of my Ballinasloe boots, Dubarry, no less — a well known Galway name — sank my heart. Flooding with disappointment, I studied him. He had an affably easy way about him, the working mouth of a cute hoor, but the long nose and the round black eyes lent him an air of bewildered innocence. I had never seen him in the flesh before.

'Jasus, Vi, me old flower, and how are you, at all, at all.'

'Hi there, Hughie; gee, it's good to see you. Hey, like you to meet my great and good friend, Jack O'Toole.'

Delaney turned to me as if I were the most important person in Ireland. He thrust out his hand.

'Arra, Jack, is it yourself? God, you're looking well, and that's the truth of it. How are they all?'

Glass in hand, I half saluted with my drinking arm. I didn't like to, but it was better than being seen shaking hands with him.

'Hello, Minister.'

'Minister, me bollocks! Will you cut out the bloody Minister; sure, aren't we all neighbour's children? Well, 'pon me word, Vi, and 'tis powerful fit and well you're looking.'

'What's coming down, Hughie?'

He rolled his eyes to the rafters, his face taking on a definite foot-of-the-cross look.

'Arra, will you stop. I'm pure destroyed these days with lachicos and gobdaws hounding and harrying me and I having a Department to run. Would you believe that I'm up in Court? Up in Court, no less; and me a member of the Government?'

'Pull the Fifth, Hughie, pull the Fifth.'

I had not listened to Brannigan for several days. Obviously, matters were proceeding apace. I might as well get it from the horse's mouth.

'Is this all the larking with An Bord Meow?' I put in.

He turned back to me like a brother in arms.

''Tis, surely. Haven't they called me down to the High Court tomorrow? Smart boyos in the wigs questioning me up and down. Sure, I'm pure destroyed.'

'That's not fair,' I said with as much emphatic insincerity as I could muster. Diaphanous as the seventh veil, a smirk crossed his face. He covered his mouth with his hand and bent over me.

'And sure I can't open me mouth.' He winked. 'Official Secrets Act. Can't say a word.'

'But, Hughie, what if the Supreme Court says you have to?'

'Won't there be a strike of the Court staff and there'll be no bloody Court?' He winked again. 'Pass no remarks.'

'Hey, you guys! Don't this little ole lady from Virginia exist any more?'

'C'mere, me old flower.'

The dirty swine had the gall to grasp the decent girl

round the waist and give her a wet kiss on the cheek. If there's one thing I can't stand, it's people with no sense of decorum, and if there's anything worse than that, it's unbridled lechery in public places. The dirty brute.

'Back off, boy; you're mussing my hair. Jack! Hughie! Let's us all have lunch!'

Delaney held up his hands.

'The Minister will bring ye to lunch. 'Tisn't every day we can entertain a beautiful foreign visitor, and 'tisn't every day I meet a sound bloody man like Jack Murphy.'

'O'Toole.'

'Aye. O'Toole. Isn't that what I'm saying?'

And that was the bitter end for me. The Church is sick sore and tired warning the people about the evils of bad companions and my Mammy didn't bring me up to have me running round the town with the likes of Hughie Delaney. Prostitutes, pimps, Mafia ladies, even the Hierarchy I will give my time to — for didn't our Saviour himself consort with Magdalen — but we are flawed and fallible and prudence is the watchword. Having lunch with Hughie Delaney was — like the probity of the banking system — out of the question.

'Look, Vi, include me out. I'm expecting Tokyo on the line and I've got to run. Sorry, Hughie.'

'Aw, come on, honey; Tokyo will keep.'

'Arra, g'way outa that, Jack. Have you a mouth on you at all? Sure that crowd are asleep at this hour.'

'No, honestly. You're very kind. But duty calls. Look, Vi, it was lovely meeting you.'

'Hey! You call me, you hear? I'm stopping over for a while.'

She grabbed my hand affectionately and thrust forward her cheek for a kiss. For one moment of witchcraft, her perfume intoxicated me and like waking from an erotic dream just a minute too early, I found myself on the street savagely cursing Delaney and making statements to myself about both his parents, his grandparents and any other person in his lineage. Forlornly, but with a new ember of hope for better days, I wended a weary way to Guinness Row. Hand on her hip, knuckles against the wall, Mrs. McGrath watched me with open mouth as I crept up the stairs and ripped the door open. Cynthia was standing up on a chair, innocently hanging a picture on the wall and Brannigan was in the grip of a furious phone call.

'But surely to Christ, ye have a fucking I.C.B.M. ye don't want? We'd pay well for it. Sure, ye must have the shed full of them.'

I motioned him briskly to cut it short. It was time for serious business and forward planning and there had been more than enough high jinks for one day. Cynthia turned to me, her eyes running me down from top to bottom.

'Ah, Jesus, Brannigan, will you look at him. Did Charlie Haughey give you one of his hand me downs?'

I am as fond of a little joke as the next man but the work of the world is not done by comedians and jesters.

'That will do, now, please. Sit down and we'll plan the next move.'

'Did he drop?' asked Brannigan heavily.

"Did who drop?'

'Adolf Eichmann.'

So that was it. Nothing on their petty little minds but money. Not a thought about the serious business in hand, but self serving, selfish interests always to the fore. I can't stand people who can't get on with it without constantly asking what's in this for me?

'Would it be any harm to remind you that the finances of this company are a matter for the board and are not to be hawked and chatted all over the floor?'

'Nice one, Jack. Would it be any harm to remind you that I'm a ranking creditor of this company and that is a matter for me and when I see the board swanning about in new suits like Gay Byrne on the Late Late Show, I'm inclined to mention the matter of my wages.'

'Jack, for God's sake will you shell out and no more about it.'

'What is it this time? Don't tell me you've gone through another pair of knickers?'

'Oh, that's him alright. Good clean family fun. Two

weeks, Jack.'

'And ditto,' said Brannigan.

There was no reasoning with them. They were small, petty people. No concept at all of the long-term view. Eat the seed potatoes and bugger next Spring.

'You'll be scrubbers all your lives,' I said sadly.

'Maybe so. But we'll be paid scrubbers.'

Both hands came out under my nose and it was the mark of my character that I didn't spit upon them. I levered out a few notes each.

'Good man, Jack. Now last week.'

Small minded, petty people. Oh, very well so. They had the temerity to actually stand in front of me and count their money. Their avarice satisfied, they lapsed into cheerier form. Cynthia pointed to the picture.

'I'm going to have my hair done like her.'

I glanced over at the wall. The frame was a cheap gilt not exceeding 50p on the open market, picked up at Quinnsworth but I couldn't deny that the photograph was a good one, artistic and expressive, obviously an enlargement bought from the *Irish Times*. It would have been churlish not to agree that the picture lent a warmth to the room and stirred a pride in me, but I had other plans for Cynthia.

'You can't. You can't have it short like that.'

'Jack, me old son; Cynthia Cockfosters will cut her hair any bloody way she likes.'

'No, Cynthia, you have to keep it long.'

'You heard me.'

'Tell her, Brannigan.'

To be fair to Brannigan, and I'm a man for credit where credit is due, he could take a point and once money wasn't involved, he had some idea of future requirements.

'Yeah, he's right, Cynthia. You'd have to keep it to the shoulders. Anyway, that wouldn't suit you at all. Wouldn't look well.'

She turned her full scorn upon the poor man.

'Are you trying to tell me that Mrs. Robinson doesn't look well? Is that what you're saying?'

'Oh Christ!' Only I would have got dandruff on my collar I would have torn my hair out. Brannigan argued on.

'No. Now, look, nobody said anything about Mrs. Robinson. All we're saying is that it wouldn't look well on you.'

'Well, now, smarty boots, I'm going to tell you something. Mrs. Robinson's hair was exactly like mine and then she cut it and look where she is now!'

'Yeah, we know all that. Point taken. But it wouldn't suit you.'

'Well, you're wrong. Her hair was exactly like mine, and now it even suits her better.'

'Ah, fuck this, Brannigan. Look, Cynthia, you're not the fucking President yet.' I am an inventive man. 'Anyway, that's a Presidential haircut. No one else is allowed have one.'

'Do you think I'm an edjit? I'm having my hair done like that and if you don't like it, Jack O'Toole, I'm sorry for your troubles.'

I sat down at the desk and covered my face in my hands. Gin can be a very depressing drink. It was Brannigan's turn again.

'Cynthia, short hair isn't on for the Blessed Virgin Mary. You wouldn't look the part.'

'I'd prefer to look like Mrs. Robinson.'

'May God forgive you. That's a dreadful thing to say.'

'I didn't mean it like that.' She paused. 'Anyway, I'm not sure about that other lark.'

'What!'

'What?!'

She stood there, head down, twisting her fingers. We stared at her. My hands began to shake and I wondered if the Dead Eyed Luciano mightn't be up on the rooftops across the street with a night sight and highpowered rifle aimed at the back of my skull. I moved smartly to another chair.

'Why not, love?' asked Brannigan softly. The silence in the room could be heard in Rio.

'Well, it's just that I'd like to have hair like her.'

Brannigan and I sat shaking our heads. But I am not only an inventive man, I am a resourceful man. You wouldn't find Sam Goldwyn sitting down and taking 'no' for an answer if he needed a certain star. No way. Old Sam would do a deal, but hell or highwater, if it was Audrey Hepburn he wanted, Audrey Hepburn he was going to get. No more than Sam, I was putting together the greatest show ever seen in these parts. Only the miracle of cinemascope was going to be big enough and the Wily Pole, the Slippery Article up in the Park or whoever the hell could, was going to pay for the overhead.

'O.K., Cynthia; I'm going to make you a deal. If you go through with this, work hard and learn your lines, do it right and leave your goddam hair alone, I'm going to do something for you. Now listen carefully. When it's all over and the job is right, I'm going to bring you down to Peter Mark, get you a Mrs. Robinson haircut, and as a bonus, I'll take you up the town and we'll get you a dress just like the one Mrs. Robinson was wearing on television the other night. Right, Brannigan, you're a witness to that.'

Her face lit up like a child at Christmas and my circulation started running again. Then a shrewd, catlike look crept into her eyes. It was a look of mercenary realisation.

'I'm a big star,' she said simply.

Brannigan looked at me warily and I looked at Brannigan warily.

'Well, sort of.'

She shook her head.

She actually shook her head.

Not alone that, she actually stood there and shook her head.

'No. I'm not going around like this any more.'

'Cynthia, don't fool around with me. I met a girl today just cut out for the part.'

'Do you still want your privates, Jack? What about the young priest? Answer me that, now.'

The most important thing about being a high player is

to know when you're beaten. No point in wriggling around. We sat in silence for several minutes and then I threw out my last card.

'O.K. Very well. O.K. I'm going to throw in an offer you can't refuse. Now, if you do, I'm going to walk out that door and I'm never coming back. So when Luciano comes round and starts burning your tits with a cigarette, you won't even know what to tell him.'

She was watching me, assessing what the traffic would allow.

'I want a promise from you now that if I throw in something else, a really big bonus, you'll leave your hair alone and go through with the whole thing. Right?'

'Is it something nice?'

'Yes.'

'And after it's over, you'll get me the hair do and the dress as well?'

'Yes.'

'That's fair enough, Jack. Provided the other thing is nice.'

'O.K. After it's all over, I'll give you a plane ticket and money and you can fly to Las Vegas and see Frank Sinatra at the Sands.'

'Is that where he is now?'

'Never leaves it. "The Fields of Athenry" every day of the week.' I had never seen her smile so beautifully. Her eyes danced and she clapped her hands.

'And the hair, Jack?'

'And the hair, Cynthia.' By God, the Church would pay dearly for this.

Chapter Six

With studied nonchalance but mounting ardour, I tripped my October evening way along Stephen's Green towards the raised twin lamps of the Shelbourne, scheming to pop in for a piss. It was more than a strategem. It was a matter of prudence and patriotism. The burdened bladder is the kind of pressure a man can do without, if he is to be mindful of his health. Many the one has needlessly punished his prostate by sitting through a Committee meeting with his knees tightly crossed and his face in neutral instead of having the moral courage to excuse himself for a minute, and damn the begrudgers — who's bladder is it anyway? We are not machines. Give the human body a fair chance to do its work and it will serve us well. Abuse the poor old warhorse and we needn't be surprised to find ourselves beset by all kinds of ill health. You can say what you like about early diagnosis, adequate nursing care and proper facilities but all these things are a drain on public funds, and there is a cogent truth in my private view that a piss in time saves nine and that proper pissing is patriotic pissing — for we all have a duty to cut back on the estimate for the Department of Health and allow the money be diverted to more fruitful purposes.

Of course, I had the scenario well worked out. By the purest happenstance, I would be tripping in the door while Vi Langley would be tripping out. We would stop, stare, and break into surprised cries of delight. 'Jack!' 'Vi, for God's sake!' A courteous hand on her warm, tanned elbow, I would guide her into the bar for a full and frank exchange of gin and tonics. As evening mellowed and the drinking worked its wiles, in for dinner; succulent roast beef and cauliflower all round. Animated conversation turning to intimacy, the wine, the lights and the music. Then, while the whole world ground its teeth in envy, fingers interlocked, we would climb the stairs to her bedroom, lock the door and what would transpire therein would cause Harold Robbins to turn his head away, blushing with embarrassment. To that intent, I walked along, my face the innocent unconcern of the interior man but a sharp lookout being kept at all times; for my heart would burst apart if, at the last moment, I saw her walking out on the arm of that well known family man, Hughie Delaney and into the back of a Government Mercedes; the dirty blaggard fondling her knee and slipping the other hand down her breasts, while whispering his foul veterinary designs in her ear. My attention was diverted by an oncoming figure I felt I should know and when he saw me, his face broke into a rapture of smiles and he hastened towards me, his hands outstretched.

'Jack, Jack, how are you?'

'Father Coddle!'

'Ah, dear, dear, Jack. You've put on a bit of weight. It suits you. How are you at all?'

'I'm at the top of my best, Father. Will you have a drink?'

He shook his head, chuckling wryly.

'Ah, God help us. Too much of that stuff and the cloth is a bad mix. Tell you what. We'll go round the corner and have a pot of tea. I know a nice, tidy place where the scones are lovely.'

My romantic visions evaporated but for some reason I didn't mind. I liked Father Coddle and half an hour in his company might well be time therapeutically spent. Anyway, I reasoned, Vi could well be lying down for her evening nap, shoes kicked off, ear plugs in and two black patches over her eyes. Couldn't I lay siege to her later on and see if fortune would be gracious?

But I did have a certain misgiving as we walked along. If there's one thing more than another which has brought this poor old country to its knees, it's the incessant drinking of tea. The whole country is tea mad. Go into any country town in Ireland and there's nothing to be seen the length of the street but tea houses and coffee shops, and even the publicans from whom one would expect better are selling cups of the same tea on the side. I remember a time when if you asked for a cup of tea in a public house, you'd be run out of it and your hat and coat thrown out on the road after you. But now it's a national aberration. Go into any Post Office. Dunta, dunta, and the one window that's opened is blocked by the intimidating arse of the mistress and she stuck into a cup of tea and the whole town waiting patiently in line for a Lotto ticket. Ring Directory Enquiries or Freephone Telecom and you'll get nothing but a recorded announcement that all the lines are engaged but please hold on. Where are they? Where are Dunta, Dunta and Dunta? Stuck in behind the partition in a body, nothing but talk of Coronation Street and the World Cup and nothing but pots of tea and Kimberley biscuits, as far as the naked eye can see on a clear day. What about a pipe burst on the main road? Out with a lorry load of able bodied men and three gangers in charge of each. Up with a little tent, the water still spewing to high heaven like a geyser. In with the lot of them and it's tea all round before they'll even dig the hole to block the traffic of the people going home from work. They have the whole country half fucked. Nobody is at their job and yet we wonder why we are going steadily down hill. Surely to God, it's not too much to expect that a man will content himself with breakfast, dinner and tea, three square meals a day like anybody else. No, begod. It's tea at eleven, tea at half three, tea going to bed, and tea getting up. The slightest excuse. An unexpected E.S.B. bill, a letter from some little upstart in the Bank or the sceptic tank backs up and what do you hear? In the name of Christ, woman; will some one of ye put on the kettle for the love and honour of Jasus! When I was a boy my Uncle Martin died roaring in agony in Greystones. My mother often took me to see him. One day in a lucid interval, he took me by the sleeve and with tears in his eyes, told me that if he had his time all over again, tea was the one thing he'd keep away from. Don't mind the drink and cigarettes, he said. It's the bloody tea that has my kidneys the way they are. I've never forgotten his words. Tea is a stimulant. It plays hell with the nerves. It stains the kidneys and the interior passageways and leaves the inside of the gullet like a stove pipe. Alcohol, for instance, contrary to what most people believe, is a depressant — keeps a man from getting all manic and jittery as Uncle Martin used to say and prayerful people will remember that it wasn't tea the Lord served up at the wedding feast of Cana. For all that, I've had my little lapses over the years for nobody is perfect but I can face anybody and place my hand on my heart, look them in the eye and claim that tea was never my sin. It was strange therefore to find myself at that hour of day, sitting in a quiet corner with Father Coddle, a pot of tea and a plate of scones between us. With an indulgent little smile, he warmed his hands on the teapot and then gave them a vigorous rub.

'Ah, God help us; that's more like it. Well, Jack, did you hear from the powers on high?'

'I did,' I said guardedly, 'matters are afoot but I'm not allowed to discuss them.'

'Well, thank God for that. I've more than enough on my plate this minute without poking my nose into what doesn't concern me.'

'Are you busy, Father?'

'Ah, you know yourself. There's a lot of suffering about. Sickness. Poverty. Unemployment. Sure I don't know how the half of them live at all and there are times I don't know myself which way to turn. Ah, dear, dear, God help us.'

'Sure, what about it? Couldn't you get your housekeeper to run the raffles and that; and all you'd have to do is say Mass, hear confessions and get on with it.

Have you a big parish?'

'Big? Not at all. Dunfeckin. Little place in the midlands.' He smiled easily to himself. 'My Bishop is a wise man and he wouldn't trust me with anything more.'

'The midlands? I thought you were a Dublin priest?'

'Not at all. God knows, I'm bad enough where I am.'

'But how did the heavy gang get you to contact me?'

'I don't know, Jack. I never heard from them before or since. I just got this phone call one day to come up and sound you out and report back.' He smiled sadly. 'I'm not much of a priest, I'm afraid, but I can run a message. But that's God's will. If God wants me to be a failure, that's what I'm going to be. Did you know that Christ was a failure — in human terms, of course?'

'Yeah. Came to a bad end. You know, I sometimes think that if he came back and saw the carry on today of his so-called Church, he'd turn in his grave. Nothing but sex, contraception, divorce and condoms on their minds. And it none of their damn business in the first place. Do they ever think about anything else?'

'Ah, God help them. They do their best. Christianity isn't about condoms. It has nothing to do with divorce and contraception. It's about love. Do you know what love is, Jack?'

'Yeah. It's about going round doing good,' I said, proud of my insight into his strange, twilight world.

'Tisn't, then. It's about saying a few kind words and five bloody minutes of your time. That's the size of it. I'm fed up of nosey people running around and doing good. Will I tell you the way I'm fixed? I'm up about a plant.'

'A plant? Geraniums for the altar, is it?'

'No, no. A central heating plant. The one below in the Church is banjaxed. You can't have people freezing to death on a winter morning. But then, if I did have the money, there's a lot more I could do with it for the poor people. I don't know what way to turn.' To my surprise, he burst out laughing. 'Ah, dear, dear. Amn't I the funny man? I'm worrying about spending money and which way to spend it — and I haven't got it anyway in the first place.'

'How much are you looking into?'

'Ha? Oh, to overhaul the lot and put it running again; sixteen thousand pounds. God bless us. I have as much chance of getting sixteen thousand pounds in Dunfeckin as you have of walking on the moon.'

I found that an intriguing imagery. It flashed across my mind that Neil Armstrong and Edwin Aldwin might have smiled too.

'Ah, well. I mustn't worry. I went into the Church this morning and spoke to God about it.'

I nodded sympathetically. It was all I could do. It was sad to think that this good man was still prey to the old, old, superstitions.

'You prayed for the money, did you?' His head shot up as if I had kicked him in the shins.

'Prayed for the money? I did not. I told him that if he wanted the Church heated he had better do something about it because, true as God, I couldn't.'

'You *told* him?'

'Of course I did. Isn't he my Father?'

'What did he say?'

'Didn't I get the notion I should go up to Dublin and get a few prices? And that's what has me here in this beautiful city today. Pass over your cup there, like a good man.'

God be good to poor Uncle Martin. At the height of his powers he was always good for a half-crown or a bag of licorice pipes and I have no doubt that that last time I saw him he rallied himself with great effort to warn me of the evils of tea drinking, for he was very fond of me in his own way, not having ever succumbed to matrimony and children of his own. I owed it to his memory to leave the tea alone. But I sat with Father Coddle that day, and while I can't be sure at this remove in time, I'd say we downed between us at least three pots of tea and the evening traffic had well thinned out when he asked the waitress for the bill. She was a well spoken girl, probably a student paying her way through College like most of the gutsy young people now-a-days, but, God help us all, her face would have blistered paint on a gate. But Father Coddle rose to her at once.

'Well, God bless you,' he said, 'but you're a fine looking girl and I'm sure you have all the young fellows running after you.' She blossomed under our very eyes for that was the way he had with him but I could hardly help thinking that if there were truth in what he said, it was her purse they were running after for certainly there was no fortune in her face.

They were burning the leaves in Stephen's Green and the old Dublin ghosts weaved in the smoke mist as in thoughtful mien I made my way along under the drizzle of the street lamps. It is an axiom of dramatic production that the first thing you get right is location. There's no point in ringing up Jane Fonda and Richard Harris and saying what about this and what about that and, Jasus, wait till I tell you; before you know where you want them. Location is all important. It matters to people. All Dublin into several postal districts divisa est. Odd numbers to the North, even to the South, each allotment of almost equal area. Dublin 18, Ballyfermot and Chapelizod. But not good enough. Up gets the crowd in Chapelizod who don't want to be lumped in with Ballyfermot and so God created Dublin 20, the size of a play pen, all for themselves. And I suppose the people of Ballyfermot preferred that too. The self same considerations applied to the undertaking which was occupying the best minds at I.E.I. All very well drafting a suitable script, coaching an actress at fabulous expense for the Main Event and not a sinner in the place with a blind notion of where the location was to be. It occurred to me that if there was a bit of business to be drummed up in a locality, an impressario of my standing could do a lot worse than turn his eyes to the peaceful bailiwick of Dunfeckin — the certainty being that if Father Coddle laid his hands on any financial fallout, it wasn't into Basilicas and bullshit it would go, but into the pockets of the poor. It might well be manners to get Thady to steal the mother's car for the afternoon some day soon and pay an incognito visit to Dunfeckin, to check the lie of the land and the possible fall of shot. I straightened my tie and, trusting providence, abandoned myself to the revolving door of the Shelbourne, a kaleidoscope of images and counter images and a bad place to be caught unless in the full pain of sobriety.

The bar was packed. If you threw a match up in the air, it could only fall on the head of some loud mouthed gobshite and you had as much chance of getting a drink as my arse has of being mistaken for the Mona Lisa.

If there's one thing which sends me climbing to the ceiling, it's brainless, uninformed comment about the evils of drink. You can't lift the paper these days without finding some doctor or psychiatrist looing and caterwauling out him about the evils of drink — and the half of them daft as a brush themselves — and not the first idea in their heads of what they're talking about — no more than the Bishops going on about love, sex and marriage. Decent drinking people have enough to put up with, what with highwayman's prices and a shilling for a breath of air, without having the bejasus scared out of them by loose talk from people who know nothing. As every thinking person realises, it isn't the drinking that does the harm but the overcrowding and shortage of barmen such as obtained at the bar that very evening. If you as much as moved a muscle to get a drink, a salacious knock-on effect ensued, causing involuntary sexual intercourse within the attendance, homo and hetero, in nature. It was a thoroughly disgusting experience. There's many the man who went yellow in the face and took to the bed not because his liver was pickled with drink but because it was pounded and pummelled in his efforts to get one. The feet, the ankles, the legs, bum and ribcage can take so much and no more. If God intended the human body to withstand that kind of abuse, he would have endowed us with an encasement of concrete instead of flesh and bone. I made a diligent hand search of all present and when satisfied that Vi was not amongst them, engaged a taxi and fled to the less rarefied but less crushed ambience of Christy's establishment. The moment he clapped an eye on me, he scurried up the bar, hands raised and palms towards me, shaking his head firmly.

'No, Jack, no. The slate is full and that's all about it.'

'Isn't that why I'm here? Didn't I clearly say, categorically and definitively that I would pay it off?'

'Aye, but when?'

'This very minute.'

His jaw fell to his chest, and his loose dentures swung perilously in the tea stained cavern of his mouth. He blinked rapidly and then, raising his eyes, crossed himself sarcastically. If there's one thing I can't stand, it's people making a laugh out of religion and I rebuked him with a sharp look. Then he recollected himself, ran to the till and produced a tatty, red covered notebook, bent at the corners like every copy of *Lady Chatterley's Lover* in the Library. In a confident, steady voice, he read aloud a total which seemed to me to be a telephone number on the London exchange. I demurred. With a conviction based on a deep faith, he repeated it firmly. I shrugged and with bad grace extracted from my nipple pocket some notes of the larger denominations. Any skilled accountant will tell you that bank interest is minimised and cash flow enhanced by denying people what is justly theirs until the very last moment, but I had a habit to feed and the lines of supply had to be kept open. With barely concealed surprise, he took my money, discharged the debit in his book and handed me the change, which by random chance, was in even notes with not a single coin. I had no loose change. I drew another note from the Papal funds at my disposal and handed it to him.

'Give us the change of that, like a good man; throw in a bit of loose change.'

He whisked it to the till, pressed the key and then his head shot up causing the neon glimmer on his bald spot to alter position. He turned in bewilderment.

'What's this, Jack?'

'What about it?'

'An eighteen pound note? I never heard of them before.'

Neither had I. I was taken by surprise but I masked it well.

'The eighteen pound note? Sure, they've been around for years. Years, man.'

'I never seen one.'

'Ah, Jasus, what are you talking about? Sure, aren't they in since the time the Europeans did away with the real money and ripped off the whole bloody country?'

It was essential that any spurious currency be exchanged for value at the earliest opportunity. Shaking his head, Christy went back to the till. He paused there and then shot me a sly, sidelong glance.

'I can only give you notes for that, Jack. Will you take two nines or three sixes?'

Seething in anger, I remained there drinking for some time. If Monsignor Casserole thought he was going to make a common edjit out of Jack O'Toole, he could think again. I already knew that the Vatican was well into forged bonds but I had not anticipated that they would have diversified into forged currency. Marcinkus was at the back of it, of course. And, apparently, he was good at it. Like all of Christendom I had not been impressed when the Wily Pole had whitewashed him by making him an Archbishop for his troubles. I resolved to contact the Nunciature in the morning and make it clear that unless financial matters were speedily placed on a proper footing, I was pulling out my team and they could look elsewhere for someone to convert the Irish people. God nose, it's not too much to ask that ordinary people will go about their business with justice and equity, paying their way, doing an honest day's work for an honest day's pay, without shirking and double dealing, trying to get something for nothing and defrauding their neighbours, which, as I understood it, was a serious violation of the Seventh Commandment and remained an encumbrance on the soul until restitution was made. Perhaps I had been naive in expecting anything better from the Church. Any institution which wouldn't mind poor old Pope John Paul the First when he was in it, and let him wake up one morning, dead in his bed, and then issue a farrago of lies to cover their dereliction of duty, quite clearly observed deplorably low standards. I was mindful also of poor old Gallileo's arm being twisted until he told lies in public about the rising of the sun to suit Church prejudice and as I drank the evening away I was beset continually by uncharitable resentments. Not a healthy mind set for the drinking man.

'Jack! Jack! It's for you.'

'Well, sign for it. I'll look at it in the morning.'

'Ah, Jasus, Jack, will you come on. It's the phone.'

It is a well established practice in Dublin public houses, affirmed again and again through the years, that if a man's wife phones looking for him, the curate will hold the phone against his tummy, count to seventy five and then reply that he is not there. If she asks has he been in, the barman will say that he has only just come on and he doesn't know. I had no wife, thank God, but the doctrine of *cy pres* should have applied and I should not have been troubled in my drinking to take a phone call. Nonetheless, Christy was standing, phone in hand, waving frantically and showing every sign of impatience. More than mystified I took the call.

'Is that Mr. Jack O'Toole?' The voice at the other end was resonant with the rich accents of a man from the county of Clare.

'What is it?' It could well have been a Civil Bill officer getting a fix on my position.

'This is the Guards in Cabra, Mr. O'Toole, and we think you may be able to help us.' Oh, sweet mother of God; they've nailed Brannigan at the dole and there's nothing surer but that he'll whistle up and I'll be spending a Christmas or two on the roof of Mountjoy, trying to get the Government to spend a little less on fancy junkets by helicopter and a little more on incarcerated men.

'Certainly, Guard. You may look to me to assist the force any time I can.'

'You're a decent man, Mr. O'Toole. Lookit, we've a young lady here and maybe you'd be able to come over and identify her for us.' Had Vi been caught while discharging a contract on some dishonest employee who had been running a hoor house in Gardiner Street and withholding the fair share due to the Mafia? It would serve my lustful intentions to come to the rescue, pay a little fine with a flourish and bear her away on my white horse to experience personally a little overflow of gratitude.

'Cabra Garda Station, is it? Let all hands bear themselves in patience and I'll be up to you within five minutes.'

I downed a glass or two to fortify myself for the exigencies of the journey across town, while Christy, embarrassingly obliging now that he had my money in the till, called a taxi. Within a reasonable time or shortly thereafter, I presented myself at the Sergeant's desk in Cabra. The station had that empty but alert stillness of the night hour and pocket radios crackled to each other as they hung along the wall, festooned with leaflets about dog licences and the evils of leaving thistles uncut.

'These bloody Americans can get awfully confused about what's what once they get abroad,' I said to the Sergeant. He looked at me uncomprehendingly.

'This is a Dublin girl we have. She has the sup taken, I'm afraid.'

'Cynthia! Cynthia Cockfosters.'

'The same. She says she works for you.'

'That's right.'

'Where does she live?'

'Dolphin's Barn.'

'Can you describe her?'

I did so. The Sergeant nodded understandingly.

'Sound enough, Mr. O'Toole. That will do us.'

'But what has she done?'

The Sergeant blinked as if he couldn't believe it himself and then shook his head at the wayward ways of a wicked world.

'Didn't we get her above in the grounds of Aras an Uactarain and she making her way cool as you please up the avenue.' He shook his head again. 'And, didn't she play pure puck when the boys tried to get her into the car. Pure bloody murder.' He stopped and stood looking sadly at the far wall. Then he bent close to my ear.

'Do you know what she said?'

I winced inwardly and my face told the Sergeant that I hardly dared to guess. He lowered his voice to the buzz of a Confessional.

'Didn't she tell the driver that if he drove her up and knocked on the hall door ....,' he glanced clandestinely about, 'she'd leave him have a feel of her tits.'

He stood back, letting the full horror of what he had said fill his face.

'Go to hell, Sergeant?'

'I'm telling you. Sure as I'm standing here.'

'I don't believe it.'

'Sure as God is in heaven this night. God, I don't know what the country is coming to at all, these young people. When I was a lad there was nothing but Whist Drives at the Parish Hall and Hopalong Cassidy on a Sunday night, and, I'll tell you another thing; there wasn't a young woman of her age between the Shannon and the sea who'd know that they had tits.'

I thought it appropriate to preserve one minute's silence. Then I nodded sadly.

'Of course, you can blame the drink for that. I'm quite shocked, because I'm going to tell you something that I don't want to go any further. Would you believe that she's head and tail of the Legion of Mary up in Harold's Cross?'

'The same bloody drink! Mind you, I knew damn well that she was a decent class of girl. That's what I couldn't understand, myself.'

I stood there eyeing the leaflets on the wall, trying hard to believe that I was hearing what I was hearing and trying to segregate fantasy from reality. There were moments when I thought I would break into a spasm of screaming in the forlorn hope of being locked up myself and insulated from a confusing world. We were facing into a major opening and the star of the show seemed intent on drawing thirty years hard labour for trying to subvert the institutions of the State.

'What will the charge be?' I asked, no longer knowing whether I cared or not. Again, the Sergeant bent confidentially near.

'Can I release her into your custody?' An ember of hope!

'You can of course, Sergeant. I'll sign any bail bond or anything like that.'

'Listen, Mr. O'Toole, you're a decent man. Can you keep your mouth shut? It's a bit embarrassing.'

'I'm like a Bank door when you're running in with a lodgement. What's the problem?'

He stared at me.

'Did you ever wonder how she got in on the gate in the first place? Answer me that, now.'

'The gate? I wouldn't be surprised if she threw her leg over the wall.'

'Well she didn't. She went in on the front gate,' he clutched my arm for reassurance, 'and the boys looking at her!'

'Looking at her?' I certainly didn't think it wise to have a crowd of drunken bowsies guarding the President and Uzi submachine guns lying loose all over the place.

'*Looking at her*,' repeated the Sergeant with heavy emphasis. 'Didn't they think she was Mrs. Robinson herself?'

I had had a fair dash that night and my mind was having trouble keeping step with history but at that very moment the impossible happened. A view down the darkened corridor from the Day Room brought me smartly to attention, tongue tied and overawed, for there coming towards us was the President of Ireland herself, a young bareheaded Guard a respectful pace behind her. I was deeply moved by what I was seeing; the tears pressing behind my eyes. This fine young woman, the best of the regal stock of Connaught, who so ably carried the destinies and dignity of a whole Nation on her shoulders, had left her official post, her duties and her family to come down late at night to give orders that no charges were to be preferred against the undeserving Cynthia. It was an incredible moment, and I was privileged to be there to witness it. Given the thugs and looderamawns that infested high office, we were blessed and fortunate to have in our highest office of all, a lady of grace, stature and impeccable integrity, and I often wondered how she managed to preserve her sanity when her daily duties brought her into contact with the sleazy politicians who were the parasites on the body politic. I was proud to be Irish that night. Frantically, I wondered what to say if she even deigned to speak to me. Was it 'Your Excellencyess' or 'Mrs. President'? I resolved to maintain a stubborn silence rather than be in the slightest way impolite. The moment she saw me, Mrs. Robinson hurried over to me. My knees began to shake.

'About bloody time, Jacko, me old son,' she said.

My ankles twisted round each other and I collapsed against the counter, the Sergeant's voice thundering over my head.

'Listen here, you, young one. Get out that bloody door with this decent man while I'm letting you, and, bejasus, if you as much as put one foot North of the Liffey ever again, I'll personally run you into Mountjoy myself.'

I cried all the way back in the taxi.

'It's my fucking hair,' Cynthia insisted.

'A deal is a deal. You did a deal, you bitch.'

'Do you think I'm gone with the fairies or something? You won't even pay for your drink. Fat chance of me getting my hair done or getting a dress out of you. As for Frank Sinatra — Jesus, don't be annoying me.'

'And where did you get that dress?'

'I signed your fucking name, mate; that's what I did. I know how you write. So, now, Jack, that's one promise you'll keep.'

'And what the fuck were you doing up in Arus an Uactarain?'

'I just wanted to show Mrs. Robinson my hair and the dress. I just wanted her to say it was alright.'

'Listen, you silly, stupid, scheming, dishonest bitch; you put your nose near Arus an Uactarain again and the

Special Branch will empty every fucking magazine they have into you. Is that what you want?'

'Well, you're wrong, smarty boots. Didn't I walk in the gate?'

'Because they thought you were Mrs. Robinson, that's why you walked in the gates, smarty boots.'

An electric silence filled the car and swelled between us and as I closed my eyes in despair, I could hear Cynthia beginning to cry softly to herself. I sat there not knowing what to do. Then her hand crept into mine.

'Jack?' All her anger was gone and her voice was small.

'Yeah?'

'Is that true?'

'What true?'

'That they thought I was Mrs. Robinson? That I really look like her?'

Suddenly I was wide awake and sitting bolt upright. Oh, sweet great fuck! Nothing would do her now but to probably ring the President to know if she could fill in on official functions if Mrs. Robinson wasn't feeling quite up to it. If Cynthia thought she could play Mrs. Robinson, she was certainly not going to settle for a minor role like the Blessed Virgin Mary. What the hell would Sam Goldwyn do if Katherine Hepburn downed tools on the African Queen and started taking singing lessons for My Fair Lady? As never before I needed a drink.

'Look, Cynthia, the light was bad; the guys were playing darts. It's a very natural mistake to make.'

'Those detectives are pretty good at spotting people. They know.'

'The hell they don't.'

'Yes they do. Jesus, Jack, I feel good.'

I didn't. As a matter of fact, I felt very bad. I took a coin from my pocket and beat the opening from Beethoven's Fifth on the window. Brannigan was in face of a pint in the cosy corner. He looked at Cynthia, swallowed hard and then smiled knowingly to himself.

'The Pride of Petravore, I suppose.'

'The pain in the privates,' I replied grimly. Cynthia laughed happily and spun herself around.

'Isn't it nice?'

'Marvellous,' said Brannigan. 'Marvellous.'

'O.K.,' I said, 'let's all stop fucking around. Now what are we going to do?'

Brannigan sat shaking his head slowly and smiling mysteriously to himself.

'Do you know your trouble, Jack?'

'Yes I do. We're into the biggest show on earth for the biggest money we've ever seen and the one, single star in the world who can play the part has fucking well gone and mutilated herself.'

'Desperate,' said Cynthia, smiling, little girl fashion, into her glass.

'No,' said Brannigan. 'Your bloody trouble is that you have no religion.'

'Look, Brannigan, just spare me any sententious bullshit at this hour. I'd appreciate that.'

'Do you ever go into a Church at all?'

'No, I never go into a Church at all.'

'More's the pity. Because if you had some bit of religion in you and you bothered your arse to as much as look at a statue, you might see something.;

'Yeah. It moving like every one in the place the year that Goofy bankrupted the country and every fucking farmer in Ireland was jumping into the Shannon.'

'I thought he was nice,' Cynthia said wistfully.

'Listen, Jack,' said Brannigan, 'in all your life did you ever see a statue of the Blessed Virgin that the head wasn't covered? Sure, fuck it, man, you could put in Sinead O'Connor and it wouldn't make a damn bit of difference.'

Chapter Seven

'Oh, God!' cried Brannigan. He clapped his hand across his eyes, fell back in his chair affecting helplessness, and then jackknifed forward and sat with his head clasped in his hands between his knees, shaking despairingly from side to side. It was an elaborate performance. I was not impressed. Rehearsals are tense and difficult for everyone, but none more so than an inexperienced actress and nothing is served by being over critical and demanding, no matter how often the same teeny weeny mistake is made. At this crucial juncture, what Cynthia needed most of all was encouragement and support in large measure and that is exactly what she was getting from me.

'Don't mind him, Cynthia — Brannigan, for fuck's sake, shut up; O.K., sweetie, just try it again, one more time.'

Cynthia stood with her back to the wall, heels together and let her arms hang down by her sides. She inhaled deeply, turned her palms forward and raised her arms slightly outward. With a nervous eye on me but with some authority she began again.

'I am,' she proclaimed boldly, 'the Immaculate Contraception.'

'Oh sweet God above in his blue heaven!' quavered Brannigan, his obsessional lust for perfection bearing him away again. I turned to him sharply.

'Look, Brannigan; this is difficult enough without any smartassed sniping from you. Now, from now on, just keep your mouth shut, a civil tongue in your arse and your comments to yourself. You're no fucking Albert Einstein yourself, if it comes to that. O.K., Cynthia, love; one more time. Go for it!'

Once again, Cynthia braced herself for the off, paused as directed and spoke her line.

'I am the Immaculate Contraception.'

She was nodding her head with every word but we could get the gestures right once the script was mastered. There is no point in pushing decent people beyond their limits, especially those who have been doing their best for over two and a half hours.

'O.K., relax everybody. Take five.' I stood up, stretched, and paced slowly round the room, my head sunk on my chest, giving myself more deeply to that creative, inspirational endeavour which draws from an actress the finest performance of which she is capable. Cynthia let out a gasp of relief, sagged with all her being and said 'Desperate'. She collapsed into a chair and lit a cigarette with shaking hands.

'Look, Cynthia, I'm going to tell you something. You are doing absolutely bloody wonderful. You're pushing out a great performance. Sometimes I've been sitting here trying not to cry. There are five words in that sentence. Four of them make eighty per cent. With that eighty per cent, you're putting out pure bloody magic. There's a sensitivity, a poignancy, a heart, a ... a ... *meaning* to it that I've rarely seen. So, don't let it get to you. Don't mind old fuckface here. You're just a tinchy-winchy shade off track on the last bit but don't mind that. We'll work at it. Every beginning is weak and Romeo didn't make it in a night and I'll tell you this — nobody looking at you would ever guess that you've never acted before in your life.'

'Then what's wrong with old fluke and worms there?'

'Just fucking jealous that we're not running a show with Saint Patrick in it as well. Look, stay where you are; we'll just get the words right. I am the Immaculate Conception.'

'I am the Immaculate Contraception.'

'You're getting there. Conception.'

'That's what I said. Contraception.'

'Ah, I see your problem. No, it's conception. Just watch my lips.'

'Yeah, I know, Jack. Contraception.'

'Conception.'

'Contraception.'

I shook my head patiently.

'No, Cynthia. Look, two different words. Two totally different things. Conception is having it off and getting pregnant. Contraception is having it off with a johnny or pulling it out; you know, like.' She gave me a dawning look, her face becoming anxious.

'Jesus, I meant to ask you about that. Do you remember the night down in Jury's; are you sure ....'

'Now, Cynthia, first things first. We'll talk about that later.'

If there's one thing more than another I can't stand it is those mercurial people who can't accept the tiny little pinpricks of the human condition without exploding into a fury and erupting in a cascade of dirty, filthy, foul, smutty words, as often as not bordering on blasphemy. The man who cannot control his tongue when thwarted by life's little disappointments is not man at all, but a helpless puppet dangling on the strings of circumstance. We lovingly rebuke those of our brothers and sisters who have so abandoned themselves in this way. Scandal is given to the innocent, sensitivities are offended and the peace of the home is set at nought. It is forgotten that all things are laid out in a tapestry of exquisite design woven by a cosmic intelligence in the craftsmanship of infinite wisdom and that even as the greasy sausage falls from its fork down the front of the dress or between the legs of the new suit, all is well and moving to an inexorable destiny and will so be seen to be. Surely to God, in a Christian country, we can all meet our little tribulations with harmless exclamations of dismay like 'Oh bother!', 'Deary me!' and 'Well heigh-ho', instead of 'Ah shit!', 'Bollocks!' and 'Well, fuck it!' and those other usages of the lower orders who know nothing better.

Haggard and wearied, Brannigan stood up.

'Ah, fuck this! Look, I've had enough. Listen, love, go down to Christy's for God's sake and have the usual waiting for us. Jack and I will be down in a minute.'

It is for the Director to say when the rehearsal is over and not the stage hand layabouts but I made no protest being somewhat worn myself from prolonged emotional input. With a grateful sigh of relief, Cynthia sprang to her feet and tripped happily to the door. With a visible heaviness of heart, Brannigan sat down beside me.

'Now, me ould son, what are you going to do now?'

'It's dyslexia.'

'Oh, motheragod,' he said, clapping his hand over his crotch in a crude but involuntary gesture, which did not go unnoted by me. 'Ah, suffering God.'

'It's not a disease, it's a condition.'

'Well, can't she take a tablespoon of cod liver oil or the weekend in bed or something?'

'Don't be fucking ridiculous. It's not a bloody disease, I'm telling you, it's a condition. She just can't tell one word from another.'

'Jasus, a girl who can't distinguish between "yes" and "no" is the handy article to have about the place.'

'She's just hung up on that one word.'

Brannigan was thinking.

'Do'y' know,' he said at last, 'I don't think it makes a damn of difference. Half the people wouldn't know the difference anyway. They'd know what she meant. Can't you let her do it in her own way? Make it easy for her?'

'And have fucking Seven Days and the *Irish Times* doing a scoop, the whole thing blown and then a Judicial Enquiry to cover it up with the Rules of Evidence , even though everybody would know the truth? Oh, nice one, Brannigan, nice. That would go down bloody well with the crowd above in the Park.

'Look, Jack, for God's sake don't mention the Park again. There'll be trouble out of that yet.' There were times when Brannigan could see something to which all the world was blind.

Thirsty men, we staggered cautiously and creaking

down the stairs. As we reached the first landing below, two enormous breasts clad in crimson emerged from the door of the flat, followed by Mrs. McGrath. Her hair was dyed jet black and her cheeks were rouged and her large mouth a neon advertisement for Berger Paints. Quite clearly, she was bent on serious business, the postman having, if the phrase be not taken amiss, come.

'How're ye, men. That's the hardy one, God knows.' She was right by pure coincidence, the climatic observations being her stock greeting, Summer or Winter.

'Brass monkeys,' agreed Brannigan in his neighbourly way.

'Aye. I seen herself going down a minute ago.'

'She's keeping a few seats warm for us.'

'Proper order. Did ye hear the place has being sold?'

'What place?'

'This place. They're saying that Hughie Delaney bought it. Aye, that's the boyo. Aye, believe me, that's the boyo. All to be pulled down and us all to be put out. He has all the rest of the street bought too. Ah, musha, God help us. Sure, Jasus, if there's anything fine and decent standing at all they'll pull it down. Glass menageries. Well, the curse of Christ on the culchie bastard and all belonging to him. They have the fucking town ruined.'

'Urban renewal,' said Brannigan. 'I'll give you anything you like that there's a Government office going up. Hughie will buy out all along the street for a song and then sell on at forty times the value to the Government. That's how they work it.'

'Well, they're not putting Lizzie McGrath out on the street, so they're not. I'm going down to the Corporation this very minute. Jasus, there's a wind out that would open a tin of salmon for you.'

'I hope it keeps fine for you, Ma'am,' said Brannigan. I had too much on my mind to give the matter further thought.

I have no time at all for these people who won't drink their quota. Far too many have died for Ireland and all too few have lived for her but far fewer still are those who drank for Ireland. Every pint raised and half one lowered lubricates the fiscal wheels of the nation. Services are provided, social welfare benefits are funded and the necessary infrastructures put in place. We must all drink our quota to make this possible. But what kind of country are we going to have unless every man jack of us puts his shoulder to the wheel and bears his share of the burden? There are far too many going home in the evening, mowing the grass or out walking Dun Laoghaire pier and shirking their responsibilities. They lounge in their arm chairs, burning foreign coal, ogling Deirdre Purcell, selfishly having nothing more than a cup of tea and a few cream crackers before going to bed. God knows, Brannigan and I had our faults. We were, at times, a little thoughtless, possibly hot tempered and coarse in our way. But no one could point a finger at us and say that we didn't drink for Ireland. We were patriots of the pint, nationalists of the naggin. In a way, I suppose, we were proud of that. We didn't ask for thanks or recognition. Amid the obscure and the unsung, we lived our lives in a humble spirit of service. We asked no reward but one. And that was that if we ever married and had children, we could face their innocent little questions and when they asked — what did you do, Daddy; we could pause with pride, leave down the knife and fork and say in a steady voice not wholly devoid of emotion: I drank my quota for my country. Because of what I did, my fellow countrymen had a finer quality of life. I ask nothing more than that.

'Do you know what's in the paper?' Brannigan asked as he slid his pint towards him and hunched his shoulder to take the weight. I inclined my head in token of my listening.

'A bloody great picture of Delaney and he above with The Slippery Article.' I noted with approval his circumspect way of not mentioning the Park with Cynthia sitting by having her morning Scotch and red lemonade.

'What are they up to now?'

'He was getting his medal from the Pope. Do you know what they did after that?'

'What did they do after that?' I asked obligingly. It was a custom between us that when the pressures allowed the news was retailed to me in form of question and answer.

'They conferred.'

I shook my head in disbelief. You can say what you like about Charlie Haughey but no way would he do anything like that. I began to speculate as to what had engaged the attention of that sinister duet but it was an idle effort, interrupted by the presence of Adolf Eichmann in the doorway, standing imperiously and jerking his head outside in summons. With studied deliberation, I got the best of the G. & T. down and ambled out.

In the far corner of the limousine, Casserole lounged in arrogant isolation. But I was determined not to lose the initiative. As I sat down heavily, he passed over a wad of notes and without thanking him I exchanged my own currency note with a stern gaze.

'Not funny.'

He arched his eyebrow and looked at it casually.

'I fail to understand you.'

'Look at it.'

'It seems a perfectly good eighteen pound note to me.'

'It's a forgery.'

'Are you suggesting that the Holy See deals in counterfeit?'

'I'm suggesting that this is a forgery and that I got it from you.'

'Am I to take it you have some expertise in these matters?' he asked with lofty sarcasm.

'You may take it that we don't have an eighteen pound denomination in Ireland.'

For a brief moment, he lost his composure. He sat forward, licking his dry lips. Then he reasserted his self possession. Fleeting as an election promise, he smiled his coffin lid smile.

'Our apologies. There has been an unfortunate confusion of documentation, and I am grateful that you drew it to my attention. The printer has blundered badly.' His face was cold as an icecap. 'He should know better. He is a prominent printer at present holidaying on his yacht in the Mediterranean. He will pay.'

'I don't care what he does so long as I'm not planted with any more of your funny money.'

'That is clear. Now, Mr. O'Toole ....'

'Doctor O'Toole ....'

'His Excellency wishes me to communicate his prayerful anxiety as to progress ....'

'Tell him we're spotting locations and conducting rehearsals ....'

He held up a dismissive hand.

'Please. We do not wish to know of your sordid workings. My mission is purely to communicate His Excellency's sense of urgency.'

'God works in his own good time.'

'I am a little more conversant with the ways of God than you are. There is another matter. You were observed conversing recently with a young American lady at the Shelbourne Hotel.'

'Yeah, I know all about her. She's Mafia. Virginia Langley.'

'No, Mr. O'Toole. Langley, Virginia, is her office address. Her name is Dorothy Schultz. Father Luciano would reprove you if anything other than purely social converse passed between you. Our business is not for the ears of the C.I.A.' He touched my knee with a skeleton hand. 'Or anybody else — including Father Coddle.'

Like those with a pathetic inability to distinguish arse from elbow or butter from margarine, I could discern no essential difference between the Mafia and the C.I.A. and the Monsignor's revelation about Vi was less than apocalyptic. I was fond of her but my only interest in her was to enlist her support in conducting a destruction test on one of the hotel mattresses. How she earned her daily bread was of little interest to me. I could also detect no difference between the American system and our own. The political and criminal worlds in either society seemed ethereally connected. A man in America will one day head the C.I.A. and direct operations involving murder, torture and blackmail. The next he will sit in the White House enthusing about the preciousness of human freedom. Another will subvert the Constitution he was sworn to protect and will fly tearfully away in a Government helicopter while the subordinates he corrupted will be marched off to prison. Given our considerably more limited resources at home, I felt that we had nothing to be ashamed of. One man will one day stand trial for smuggling arms. The next day he will head the Government. Another will be under investigation by the Fraud Squad for certain land deals, and then, in a turn of the political wheel, find himself beyond their scrutiny as Minister for Justice. In both countries, those in power will draw around them a coterie of financial thugs and corporate gangsters to whom they will offer a cut from the public purse in return for contributions to party funds and other little favours difficult to discern. Their perks and pensions, their institutionalised tax evasions, opulent lifestyles, will be screwed from the paypackets of those foolish enough to work, who struggle to keep their homes intact and their bowels regular by a good fibrous diet of sugared cardboard, alias cornflakes, on the table. In the event of a contretemps, snafu or cockup, the powerful ones will proclaim their ethics and high standards while the innocent Civil Servant who railed through the years against what was going on would be disgraced and forced to resign. No solace could be expected through the Democratic process. In the event of an electoral upheaval, Raheny Rogues would be replaced by Donnybrook Dilettantes, who, crying for fiscal wrecktitude, would double the National debt, cream off nineteen per cent pay increases and distribute as much as they could amongst their own little playmates. Stability was taken to mean that nothing changes. But we are, thank God, a docile people for I sometimes feared that if we didn't have football, racing and a bit on the side to keep us amused, blood might flow on the streets. Being a peace-loving man, I tended to be philosophically indifferent to public affairs and the only thing to which I did advert in

Monsignor Casserole's allocutio was the chilling reference to Father Luciano and the necessity to keep one's mouth tightly shut at all times.

On a bright day of clement weather, Thady — he of the polished American accent — immobilised his mother by putting California Syrup of Figs in her tea and confined her to her bed for long enough to purloin her split screen Morris Minor and drive us to the sleepy village of Dunfeckin. Brannigan, who didn't drive, sat in the front telling Thady how, and Cynthia and I sat in the back, her hand straying thoughtlessly from time to time up my thigh and trespassing on my fertile ground, until I had cause to fear that the Private Member would leap from his lair and smite Brannigan in the ear. Dunfeckin was little more than the small old Church, a cluster of small houses, a post office which doubled as a would-be supermarket and thirty-six pubs. The terrain was flat and featureless and away in the distance the Shannon waters gleamed in the sun and the many mushroomed watertowers of distant Athlone. We passed through the village and began to survey the outer environs. Dank, low lying fields adjoined the road, most of them bearing posted warnings that the lands had been preserved for the local Gun Clubs. These, apparently, indulged themselves in the delightful sport of handrearing pheasants which grew up tame until when the season opened they obligingly walked towards the guns to give themselves up and had the shit blown out of them at two yards range. The road snaked and curved through a series of enormous potholes and there were times when Thady had to lighten the car in order to drive it out of one.

'We're looking for some old ruin,' I said.

'There's one,' said Thady rather tastelessly as he damn near collided with an old man drunkenly cycling his bicycle on the crown of the road, his ears incongruously encased in a Walkman.

'It's got to be in a remote place, but somewhere where children play. I've read up on this kind of thing and that's the form.'

In fact I was beginning to hope that our assignment might be easier than anticipated. Some years previously, a flickering candle light had played on the face of a statue of the Virgin and within weeks devout people had done the rest. It was difficult to find any statue which wasn't alleged to be moving and the few which weren't began to bear placards 'Out of Order'. At the same time, it wasn't all that easy. Competition was keen. Our little show had to be singular and dramatic if we were to avoid a plethora of competing little sideshows in every Parish in the country. I had already raised with Monsignor Casserole the unwillingness of the Bishops to endorse these manifestations. I thought their silence strange, given their penchant to rush into print on matters they knew nothing about.

'Leave the Bishops to me,' he had said grimly. 'The Bishops will say what they're told to say.'

The road curved again in a sickening semicircle and a tiny schoolhouse came into view. A small water tower stood at one end and a muddy football field lay beside it. In the next field, a gutted old stone barn stood. There was a loft above with an imposing opening.

'Thady, stop the car.'

'I'll come with you.'

'You can't. Stay with the car. They knock them off and eat them down here if you don't watch them.'

There was no-one about as we trudged down a lane in the opposite direction to mislead Thady, and we approached the old barn from the rear.

'Jasus, me shoes are wringing,' said Brannigan who had never been west of the Lucan Spa Hotel in his life and thought that wet grass was purely decorative.

'Desperate,' said Cynthia, clinging on to his arm.

My hawk like features immobile, I looked about in a gimlet manner. With the exception of one or two preowned contraceptives on the floor, there was no sign that anybody frequented the place. The straw was old and moulding and any cow turds were well seasoned. The air within was warm and redolent of stale oats. Access to the upper floor was gained by a surprisingly sturdy ladder. The loft was half filled with old dead hay and the opening gave out onto the football field. Allowing for the primitive conditions, Cynthia's chum Mr. Sinatra would have found it excellent for a concert. I could hardly believe our good fortune.

'Listen, me old son. Supposing we were at our little prank and the crowd rushed us. How would we get away? Did you ever think of that?'

I had.

'We bundle into the hay and when the search party comes up, we mingle with them with angry shouts of "we'll get the fuckers yet".'

Brannigan looked at me with some admiration. Cynthia didn't.

'There's no way I'm going to jump into that stuff. No way.'

'Now, Cynthia, this will be your finest hour.'

'Ah, Jack. Will you look at the cut of my shoes. Jesus, just look!'

I waved her aside.

'Don't worry. Although you went back on the deal, I won't. I'll still get you another dress and I'll throw in a pair of shoes as well.'

Her eyes widened.

'You will?'

'Of course I will. Now stroll around and get familiar with the place. There's going to be thousands of people here soon watching you. Keep well away from the window, though.'

Her wide eyes widened some more.

'Jesus, I'll be just like Mrs. Robinson.'

'Mrs. Robinson wouldn't get a show like this.'

'Oh, Jack.' She wandered about and we saw her enthusiasm grow. She kept shaking her head in wonder, clapping her hands lightly and twirling round like a ballerina. For the first time I began to be confident her heart was in it. Then her lips began to move as she whispered her line, until with a delighted expression she turned to us.

'Jack, you won't believe this. I've worked it out. I

know how to say the line. Oh, it's wonderful.'

Her joy could not be contained. Even though it was getting late and drinking time was on us, I decided to take the tide in flood and encourage her.

'Look, Cynthia; keep away from the opening. But Brannigan and I will sit here and you go over there and give us a show.'

'Oh, I'd love that. Now, you two keep very quiet. You're not to say anything.'

Totally relaxed I placed my bum on a haybale while, somewhat more cynically, Brannigan sat beside me. Cynthia went over to the far wall. She stood absolutely still, obviously psyching herself into the part. Then, head erect, standing like a Queen, she took one graceful step forward. With no trace of nervousness, she slowly turned the palms of her hands towards us and drew her arms outwards like rays of sunlight shining down. I could only bite my lip to contain myself. Then in a firm, clear voice,

'I am the Immaculate Family Planning.'

Chapter Eight

Some men are wise and some are otherwise.

I had nipped in to the Shelbourne for a peremptory piss when Hughie Delaney accosted me in the foyer.

'Jack O'Toole, me decent friend, c'mere til I have a word with you.'

I felt chagrined. The political creature has his den at Leinster House. In that comfortable environment, insulated from the realities of life and the real world of an honest day's work for an honest day's pay (less tax, P.R.S.I. and V.A.T.), he enjoys his subsidised meals, duty-free booze, free post and phone calls and he has no business emerging on the town where decent people may have to rub shoulders with him. Is there nowhere safe that a man can't run in to have a piss without having to mingle with undesirables who greet him with a guffaw, pass themselves off as old friends in the full view and hearing of the passing populace? Nonetheless, overcome by curiosity and with ever the eye for the main chance, I allowed myself be taken by the elbow to the bar, hoping to get drunk enough not to care whether anyone saw us together or not.

'What about d'ould rent, Jack?' Delaney murmured out of the corner of his mouth, after I had been gracious enough to allow him present me with a gin and tonic.

'What rent?'

'D'ould office beyond. You haven't paid it for months.'

I did not like my financial business coming to the knowledge of someone like Hughie Delaney.

'But what has that to do with you?' I asked with some

understandable asperity. A devious smirk crossed his face and disappeared.

'Well, like, the place beyond is owned by a friend of mine. He just happened to mention it, like.' He covered his mouth with his hand, cornerboy like, and bent closer. 'Tell me, Jack, are you in some kind of trouble or something?' I dismissed this with a careless laugh.

'Is there anything I can do for you, at all, at all?' Delaney enquired. I did not know what he meant. I shook my head.

'There isn't an ould drunk driving summons I could square for you or anything like that?'

'No.'

'Or maybe, there might be an ould Income Tax bill we could tear up?'

'No.'

'What about an ould Grant, like? Or, maybe, would you like to be fixed up with a good job? Like, couldn't we put you on the Board of something or other. £500 a year, taxable, and £30,000 expenses, free of tax? Sure, Jasus, like, maybe, like, we could throw in a car?'

He mystified me. The man owed me nothing and yet he was childlike in his anxiety to smoothen my path in life. I wondered for a moment until some deep thinking made me remember that a politician is always on the make and doesn't offer his help for nothing. It occurred to me that he might be unsettled by a direct question.

'What do you want, Hughie?' I asked bluntly.

The Irish politician is not used to people coming to the point. They live in a world of wink and nod, the veiled innuendo and deniable suggestion. Words mean what they say they mean and they suffer unduly from misquotation by the media. For all that, if there are no witnesses present and nothing is in writing, they will engage in an open conversation provided that they can later give, on mature reflection, a categorical, unqualified, absolute assurance that no such conversation ever took place. Delaney lifted his glass and deliberated slowly if it might be wise to answer my question. A long term crafty look passed over his face.

'I believe,' he said at last, looking innocently into the middle distance, 'that we have a mutual friend above in the Park?'

'The President?' I asked, wondering what Mrs. Robinson might say if accused of being a friend of Hughie Delaney. He winked.

'You're getting warm, Jack.' I froze. But I needed to hear more. I turned on him an innocent gaze, guileless as his own.

'Go on, Hughie. I'm listening.' He put his mouth uncomfortably close to my ear.

'Great things are expected, Jack, I hear. All I want to know is where?'

So that was it. Archbishop Cojones had his reasons for confiding in Delaney. The Nuncio was twice as devious as any politician and it was a waste of time wondering what his motives might be.

'I don't know what you're talking about,' I said in a full and frank manner, 'but why might all that be of interest to you?'

A look of extraordinary candour came over his face. I had seen it before on television and it usually heralded the telling of a studied lie. The headquarters of all parties expended large sums of money in having their members coached in the arts of looking candidly into the cameras and telling lies or evading the point by answering questions they had not been asked. Hughie's face was a study in sincerity and frankness.

'Well, Jack; you've asked me a straight question and I'll give you a straight answer. I'm an honest man and I have nothing to hide. I'll tell you the way it is, like. You see, if there was anything going on, t'would only be right if it was below in the Constituency. Land is very cheap down there at the moment, if you follow me. And that's the truth of it, Jack.'

I had great difficulty keeping my face schooled in the childlike innocence of his own. Delaney represented the Constituency of Ireland Central, a sprawling midland triangle which took in the tiny village of Dunfeckin. Any dramatics there could be exploited to his benefit. I would not want that but I was somewhat underjoyed at the prospect of having to go into the highways and byways to find a new location.

'I see,' I said slowly, nodding to myself. 'Now, Hughie, that's very interesting. Very interesting, indeed.'

'Aye. Of course, you'd be in there yourself, Jack, for d'ould five per cent.' His voice sank to the murmur of a penitent in prayer. 'Pass no remarks.' His face lightened with that far away visionary look and deep spiritual joy of the politician who sees at last how the public interest can be reconciled with his own. He ran his eye unseeingly round the room.

'D'ye know,' he remarked casually, 'I could see a great, bloody big airport being built there yet.' He looked at me again as if he could at last see a way to help me. 'And you'd be in on that, Jack, for five per cent. Bejasus, that wouldn't be bad for you now, so it wouldn't.'

I considered this in silence, aping his own casual unconcern.

'Tell you what, Hughie,' I said brightly, 'if I hear anything at all, you'll be the first to know.'

He nodded like a man whose word was his bond and seized me warmly by the elbow.

'Didn't you know you were a sound man? 'Pon my word, I said to myself, Jack O'Toole is one sound man. That's exactly what I said to myself when I met you. Now, tell me this; one more thing, how are they all at home?'

I had no home and there was no 'they'.

'Never better, thank God,' I said.

'That's all I wanted to hear. Once I hear them people is well, I don't care who's sick.'

Tidings of great joy were waiting for me back at Guinness Row.

'She's got it,' said Brannigan jubilantly. 'Show him, Cynthia.' Like a child anxious to perform a party piece, Cynthia took up her position at the wall. Her face lit up with an angelic glow.

'I am the Immaculate Conception.' She announced solemnly. It was flawless.

'And what are you not?' pressed Brannigan encouragingly.

'I am not the Immaculate Contraception, and I am not the Immaculate Family Planning,' said Cynthia obligingly. A flicker of doubt wakened in my mind.

'You wouldn't want to actually say that, Cynthia,' I said.

'Oh, I know,' she said, smiling as if the idea had never crossed her mind. I was more than pleased. A great production breakthrough had taken place. There is a time to ease springs and reward the diligent labourers.

'I think we deserve a drink,' I said magnanimously, mindful of poor old Uncle Martin who always claimed that the odd indiscretion was no harm.

The midday sun slanted warmly along the bar of the Cart and Horse but as a wind was scything down the street and gaining entrance on the doorway, we took our stand down at cosy corner, reflecting that God was good and there was no need to keep an anxious eye on the office door. The only other occupant at that hour was Mrs. McGrath who had spread her voluminous arse on the middle stool and was in close communication with a pint which nestled within the marvellous cleavage of her tits.

'That's the hardy one,' she remarked as usual, and if she had said anything else I would have run into John of Gods by evening.

'How did you get on with the Corporation, Ma'am?' asked Brannigan in his chatty way.

'I gave them what for,' she said grimly. 'Bejasus, the Corporation know where they stand with Lizzie McGrath.'

'Are they pulling the place down?'

'And indeed, they are not and Hughie Delaney isn't either. The place is a preserved building. And sure why the feck wouldn't it, and Lizzie McGrath living in it this thirty years?'

'Has Hughie bought it?'

'It's a Company that has bought it,' answered Mrs. McGrath, pleased at being the bearer of up to date intelligence. 'Suppository Securities of the Isle of Man, no less, if you please. That would be the bould Hughie's style alright.'

Apart from the postman's, there were no flies on Mrs. McGrath.

'Will you have a drink, Ma'am?' I asked. She looked at me with a new appreciation of my validity as a human being and a sober citizen in good standing.

'Well, bejasus, I will and thank you very much Doctor O'Toole, for I've the ague bad this weather and the Doctor says I have to take plenty of liquids. Isn't Hughie the horrid hoor, just the same?'

'A hoor's ghost,' I said.

'A prostitute's winding sheet,' Brannigan said.

'Desperate,' said Cynthia, still flushed from her dramatic triumph. Her Mrs. Robinson's dress looked a small bit tatty as she had never taken it off since the day she had acquired it at my expense. Christy sidled up to me, funereal of face.

'The slate, Jack. It's beginning to look a bit bad again.'

'Fear not, Christy. Even at this very moment, various irons in the fire are glowing red and you and I will be little older before land is in sight and all will be well. I do wish you wouldn't worry about these paltry little matters.'

'The total on the slate doesn't look like a little matter to me.'

'Jesus, you're a terrible man. You have no sense of proportion at all.'

If there's one thing I can't stand, it's people not trusting one another. God nose, if we cannot trust each other and behave as brothers, what right do we have to call ourselves Christians? Where would the country be if everyone was obliged to pay their debts on the nail? All commercial life would grind to a stop, people would start living within their means which would be disastrous for production and distribution and many the decent person would be thrown out of work. Only the banks seemed to understand that. They were opening holes in the wall, advertising widely with smooth young yuppies pushing money across the counter to encourage debt, and being friends for life and allowing us to bring out the best in them, all so that people could live beyond their means and keep the economy stimulated. If people like Christy were allowed indulge their neurosis, the whole country would go out of business, and he seemed to have no idea at all that he was striking at the root of the National interest.

'My bank manager doesn't like me running credit,' he moaned.

'That's because he likes to run credit himself and he doesn't like people getting in on the act. The loan shark, whether backstreet or High street doesn't like competition.'

I resolved to put my economic theories on paper some time and give Garrett Fitzgerald something other than theology to think about, it being essential to the aforesaid National interest that he be kept on the back benches as God intended and not be developing notions of going for office again, which would be more than the country could stand. I was pleased to realise that much of my thinking was public spirited and unselfish. Christy slunk away with a disobliging look on his face, not a bit of appreciation for the fact that the slate had been cleared before and that business people cannot be squandering liquid assets by paying debts all the time. I turned to my companions and expressed the view that he was a whore in his heart.

'Thady was in great voice today,' Brannigan said.

'Yeah?'

'He's all on for a dozen helicopters, air to ground missiles laid on and he's thinking over whether he'll throw in a few chemical warheads on the side for luck.'

Fair play to Brannigan, he took these phone calls very seriously and I could only hope that the Special Branch was listening attentively and not lying about reading the *Star*. To have the phone cut off wouldn't do and we about to reach the climax of our operation.

'Sunday week is opening day,' I announced.

'Sunday week!' they exclaimed in unison.

'Sunday week.'

They began a faint-hearted, cowardly clamour.

'Sure, Jasus, Jack, we're not ready. What about lights? Was about a costume? Jasus, you're a desperate man for going off at half cock.'

I surveyed them with derision.

'Do you think I haven't thought of all that? Do you seriously think I haven't been out and about attending to these little details?'

'What about the costume?' asked Brannigan, his glass midway to his lips and his mouth hanging open in a distrustful manner.

'That's your problem. I've enough to do what with directing and the lights.'

'Wha'?'

'Costume is your problem.'

He began shaking his head in a disobliging, hangdog way.

'Ah, now, lissen, Jack, me old son; fair is fair. Where would I get the Blessed Virgin's hand-me-downs?'

With that razor sharp mind which fascinates all who know me, I told him.

'Isn't your mother a member of the Sodality above in Rathmines?'

'And what has that to do with anything?'

'Hasn't she a nice sky blue cloak and a white veil? Tell me this, Brannigan, do you ever go into a Church at all? Did you ever see the Virgin Mary wearing anything else?'

His mouth closed slowly and he gave me a long, long look.

'Jesus, you're the cute hoor and no mistake.'

'Amn't I just? Steal, purloin, make away with it. Self drive. We'll bring it back.'

'And you better. I'm not having the mother going to hell for all eternity just because she couldn't say her prayers. Oh well, game ball. A hundred quid a night, Jack, old son.'

'What?'

'A hundred quid a night. To hire of costume. We'll say

nothing about the V.A.T.'

I was speechless. How mercenary minded people cannot oblige a friend without bringing money into it is more than I can understand.

'You're not telling me that you're looking for money?'

'Jasus, Jack, you're very quick on the uptake, I'll say that for you.'

I shook my head like a man confronting nemesis.

'Ah, come on. I might go twenty just as you're a friend.'

'I'm sure you would. A hundred. If yer one's frilly knickers is worth fifty, a slightly used Virgin Mary outfit is worth a hundred.'

'Leave my knickers out of this,' said Cynthia indignantly, catching the last few words.

'Gladly,' said Brannigan, the smutty beast. 'Now, Jack, take it or leave it.'

Mrs. McGrath cackled happily to herself as the drink took hold of her.

'Hey, why did the Corkman use two contraceptives?' she roared up the bar. I turned away. I will have no smut or dirt in my company and I wasn't interested in her agricultural wit.

'Why?' said Cynthia before anyone could stop her.

'To be sure, to be sure,' said Mrs. McGrath, cackling delightedly at her own joke.

'That will do, Madam,' I said. It was very distracting trying to plan operations with Mrs. McGrath running her offensive little burlesque from the touch lines. She couldn't be stopped.

'Hey, why did the feminist cross the road?'

'Don't answer the old bitch,' I warned them.

'Why?' said Brannigan, the faithless wretch.

'Why the fuck shouldn't she?' howled Mrs. McGrath. She rocked precariously on her stool, her ample bosom quivering in time to her jollity. 'Ah, sure, Jasus, God help me, I'm in great form, so I am. Sure amn't I after getting a free ticket to Teneriffe and the money to stay there on the post from a mystery admirer? I'm off a Saturda'.'

'Any admirer of yours could only be a mystery,' I shot back. But there was no downing her.

'Ah, now, Jacko, pure jealous you are that I wouldn't bring you.' She cackled again as the blood ran cold in my veins.

'What about the lighting?' asked Brannigan. But I had foreseen everything.

'Haven't I been up to this fellow on the Long Mile Road and I've hired out a portable flood lamp with a dimmer and a backpack?'

'A what?'

'A backpack. You carry it like a knapsack. That's where the battery is. They use them for shooting outdoor films. The dimmer is so that we can bring the lighting up and down slowly. None of your old click on and off, only disturbing the simple faith of the people.'

'Shut up, will ye,' snapped Christy, inserting one finger deep in the wax of one ear and trying to listen on the phone with the other. With a surprised look, his eyes travelled down the bar to me. He jerked his head. I took the phone cautiously.

'Hi there, Jack O'Toole. Why didn't you call me, you naughty boy?'

'Vi.'

'Right. Where have you been, stranger? Hey now, why don't you come round here? I've been getting kinda lonely.' I formed the view that she had drink taken and was unfit to drive. It's a terrible thing to think of foreign girls staying in our hotels, crying out for the company of an able bodied man and the same fellows hanging round the bars doing nothing but drinking. It's no wonder that the tourist industry is on the slide with half the people not pulling their weight. When Ireland of the Welcomes calls, Jack O'Toole will not be the man to be found wanting.

'I'll be round in a minute. Take up a pole position in the bar.'

'I'm in the goddam bar, honey.'

The Private Member rose like a giraffe stretching for the most succulent leaves at the top of the tree as with an airy carelessness I strolled back down the bar. Mrs. McGrath gave me a lecherous wink as I passed; the same old bat not being half as drunk as she was pretending.

'What was that?' said Brannigan, never the one to mind his own business if he could.

'I'm cultivating a client,' I said mysteriously. 'This might give rise to something big. Now what about Cynthia's lines? Is anything being done about that?'

Brannigan put his hand into his inside pocket and pulled out a sheet from a shorthand jotter.

'I've been drafting something,' he said. I was pleased that he had been giving the project some little attention.

'Read it.'

He pushed back his glass and squinted at the paper. Then he cleared his throat and read slowly:

"There's to be no more contraception or anything like that. I don't want any more talk about divorce and yiz are all to go to Mass every Sunday. There's to be no more selling of rubber johnnies in the shops or dirty films on T.V. I am very cross. It will rain for forty summers if yiz don't stop."' He looked up, pleased with himself. 'That's the sort of thing we want,' he said.

'Am I supposed to learn all that off,' asked Cynthia incredulously. It was a good question. It had taken three weeks to get her to master five words.

'I'll say this for you,' I said, 'it's a hell of a try. But I get this vague feeling that we're missing some authentic nuance. I don't think the Blessed Virgin would speak like that.'

'Couldn't we get Mrs. Robinson to give a speech?' asked Cynthia, warming visibly to her own idea. Brannigan rolled his eyes in painful patience.

'Look, Cynthia; if you don't mind. We'll just keep Mrs. Robinson out of this for the time being.'

'Well, I think she should be there,' Cynthia said firmly. I shook my head equally firmly.

'You have no consideration, Cynthia; I'm ashamed of you. There's that good woman on the go, night, noon and morning and nothing will do you but to overload her schedule. Do you want the poor woman to collapse altogether?'

'She wouldn't mind,' Cynthia said.

'That's the trouble. She wouldn't. She's far too good. Now, Cynthia, just try to think of her wellbeing. We must try to do something for ourselves, without expecting Mrs. Robinson to do everything.'

'I suppose,' said Cynthia doubtfully. I was a foolish man to think she she had left the idea there.

Vi Langley looked far more radiant than I remembered her. Tall and feline in a tan safari suit, she flashed me a welcoming grin as I took the stool beside her, having stood for some moments behind the former occupant, scratching vigorously and muttering aloud that the same A.I.D.S. had me pure destroyed.

'Hey now; you're looking well,' she said dreamily.

'I'm feeling well,' I said with every regard for truth.

For some cosy hours we poured out our hearts to each other, speaking of this and that and that and this and some other things as well. Vi said that Ronald Reagan was the best thing that had ever happened to the United States. I told her how Garrett Fitzgerald had engineered an Honorary Doctorate from Galway University for him in, of all things, International Law; and she laughed and laughed about that until her straw gold hair fell forward into her glass. She then told me about Richard Nixon spending his last hours in the White House when lie after lie had failed him and how he then consulted with Kissinger and they had fallen to their knees in the Oval Office to pray; and I laughed and laughed about that, until my dandruff started falling like snow all over the counter. I then told her how John F. Kennedy's likeness was enshrined on the wall of Galway Cathedral because he symbolised the good, Catholic family man, and she laughed and laughed and started fondling my knee and saying 'I don't believe you, honey; I just don't believe you.' Then I told her the one about the four train robbers who bet the shite out of themselves, ran into Court at midnight and signed confessions after the heavy gang did no more than read them fairy stories all day and serve them up tea and swissroll and how the High Court and Supreme Court could see nothing odd about this at all, at all; and she laughed and laughed so much and kept saying 'Jack, you're kidding; you're kidding, Jack' until our faces came within an inch of each other and she looked at me and I looked at her and our hands clasped and we kissed as if the whole goddam bar was empty.

'Hey now,' she whispered like a summer breeze wandering through a hay field, 'what the hell are we doing sitting here?'

And I said, '

'I was beginning to ask the same question myself.'

And she said,

'Hang around, honey; I'll go and get my key.'

And like lovers in a dream, we joined hands and tried to trip lightly up the stairs four times until I said 'Well, fuck this for piano playing' and we picked ourselves off the floor again and went up in the lift.

If there's one thing I can't stand it's dirty, filthy, disgusting books where lewd things are depicted and narrated in obscene detail. This type of farmyard literature incites innocent readers to impure behaviour and what's more, enkindles in them expectations of sexual intercourse which have no basis in fact; giving them a totally false idea of what obtains between normal, chaste, married couples. This is the kind of thing which should be put down with a strong hand. Purely for example, and not for titillation, I quote now a mercifully brief extract from a book which I felt constrained to seize from a six year old on the bus the week before. It is a paperback with a lurid cover showing a highly suggestive snowman, plagiaristically entitled 'The Iceman Cometh'.

'Tilly lay on her bed moaning with pleasure. Languidly, she extended one heel on to the window cill and the other on the dressing table as the warm succulent crevice of her sexuality parted slowly like curtains being drawn back in a crematorium, her public hairs crackling

with static. Roger covered her avidly as his engorged member rose like the fore armament on a dreadnought class cruiser and trembled between her thighs and he entered her with a plopping noise like the horizontally opposed piston of a Volkswagen engine; throbbing in and out as if the rings were slightly worn. Her screams of pleasure mounted, inciting him to higher revs, his buttocks rising and falling in powerful strokes like the big end bearing on a Marine diesel. '"Oh yes! Oh God, oh yes," she cried, her nails biting into his back like a JCB clearing the pimples from his skin. His hoarse roars of delight mingled with hers until in a final crescendo, their passions burst together and they sank into that blissful valley of tranquillity that only lovers can know and the frenzied pounding on the bedroom wall ceased with a final angry roar "For fuck's sake, will yiz be quiet in there, the children are trying to sleep."'

That's the kind of filthy, disgusting literature the Church is against and rightly so. Why people can't read *Our Boys* and *A Tale of Two Cities* like long ago, I can't understand. Uncle Martin often said that there was no sex or television in his day and he got on just as well without it. As any mature married person knows, the reality of sexual encounters, if they must take place, is totally different.

'Ah gee, honey.'

'You keep doing it, I'll be alright in a minute.'

'No, honey; let's go asleep. We'll try again in the morning.'

'No, honest to God; I'm just out of breath. Just keep running your fingers over it.'

'But gee, honey, it's like trying to stuff a marshmallow into the slot of a piggy bank!'

'Tell you what, I'll just keep tweaking your tits.'

'Ah hell, honey, I'm sore.'

Vi sat up against the pillows, her honeygold hair falling over her face. She cuddled my head and laid it warm against her breast. Dreamily, her voice came to me from long, long away.

'Hey, Jack. Can I ask you something?'

'Sure.'

'What kind of a guy is your guy, Brannigan?'

'Brannigan? He's alright. Kind of fond of money and a bit greedy, but he's alright.'

'Does he do anything else outside working for you?'

'I sometimes doubt if he even does that. No. He lives with his mother. Not married or anything odd like that.'

'What does he do after hours?'

'Drinks and takes the mother to bingo.'

'Is that all?'

'I think he makes the odd lunge at Cynthia. I've noticed things. What put all that into your head?' I was half asleep and I don't remember if I even heard her reply.

'I don't know. I just sorta wondered, I guess.'

Chapter Nine

At prodigious expense, I hired a taxi and made my way clandestinely to the quiet midland village of Dunfeckin. I was in need of spiritual consolation and bethought that a private visit to Father Coddle in his native habitat might provide the solace which my soul required. The presbytery was a modest old house in the church grounds, a handball alley having been built against the gable wall. A few sturdy country youths were at their play, their boyish shouts of 'Bollocks' and 'Oh shit' giving testimony to their enjoyment of the game. Father Coddle opened the door himself and welcomed me into the kitchen. Quite clearly he was alone and fending for himself.

'Where's your housekeeper, Father?' I asked, concerned for his welfare.

'Ah, Mrs. Lucey, is it? Sure, I couldn't afford to keep her. She got a job round the Courts with some crowd above in Dublin. I'm looking after myself quite well.'

He wasn't. The kitchen was full of dirty dishes and the fire in the stove was almost out. I did not think it my place to say anything.

'Are you busy these times?' I asked. He nodded, his face troubled.

'Ah, Jack, people go through terrible suffering at times. I don't know what to do. There's a poor widow beyond and she hardly has the bit to put in her mouth. And the gas of it is that she has over two thousand acres and she can't sell it.'

'What sort of land is it?' I really didn't care but I knew from watching Glenroe that that's the kind of civil question to ask if anybody mentions land.

'Pure snipe grass and scrub. Nobody would want it. You could do nothing with it.'

The ghost of poor Uncle Martin rose before me as he wet a pot of tea and we sat drinking together at the kitchen table, munching toast.

'Did you ever do any good with the central heating, Father?'

He shook his head sadly and then he brightened up.

'God is good, Jack and he works his wonders in his own good time. Paddy Coddle would be a better priest if he remembered that. How are you keeping yourself, tell me?'

'Fine thanks, Father.'

'And business is good with you?'

'Never better,' I said gratefully, Monsignor Casserole having called the night before and unloaded some more Christian charity. I was mindful that Robert Maxwell had disappeared over the side of his yacht in mysterious circumstances.

As to Father Coddle, I couldn't make head nor tail of this simple man. There he was in the arsehole and armpit of nowhere, up to the ears in problems and still placidly bearing himself with cheerfulness. I wondered about his God to whom he prayed so ardently. I began to wonder if God was not getting too old and whether a younger man shouldn't be brought in. These blasphemous thoughts occupied me for some time as I chatted to him in a preoccupied way. Suddenly, like that well known feminist of old who was thrown from his horse on the road to Damascus, I was stricken by a blinding light. I could not believe that the obvious was so obvious. The only question was if Father Coddle's faith was equal to the occasion.

'Father, I've something to say to you.' He nodded calmly.

'Tell me as much as you like, Jack, and as little as you like. You'll be the better for getting it off your chest.'

'Father, I want you to buy up all the poor widow's land. If you pay her slightly over the odds, she'll have enough to live on and you'll make enough to run your parish and look after your people.'

He shook his head, laughing happily at a dream.

'Ah, God bless your head, Jack. Sure if the bank gave me as much as the deposit, that would be all. And, sure, I could never pay it back.'

'You could.'

He laughed happily to himself at the very idea.

'But how, Jack?'

'Take an option on all her land and sell it on at once.'

'Sell it, Jack? Me dear man, you couldn't give it away if you went down the town handing it out in buckets.'

'You could.'

He shook his head wondering at me.

'Ah, dear, dear, Jack, I wish that could be. It's like all the wonderful ideas; it wouldn't work.'

'That's what they told Marconi. And Edison. Maybe they told God that when he made the world.' I wondered were they right about that.

'Jack, what's come over you at all?'

'I know what I'm saying. Father Coddle, I want you to trust me. I want you to go out and get an option on the land, signed sealed and delivered and ring me the minute you have it done. I promise you it will work. You'll have the land sold on within the fortnight at three times the price.'

'Three times?'

'Make that five. We'll be playing into a ready market. But you must move immediately. There's not a moment to lose.'

He sat there with his cup in his hand, smiling up the table at me and shaking his head slowly.

'Oh ye of little faith,' I said sadly, knowing damn well that words to that effect appeared somewhere in his breviary. He sat there in silence for the longest moment I have ever known. Then he smiled to himself, shaking his head again. He seemed to be looking at me and far past me at the same time. Suddenly he left down his cup and straightened himself.

'Now, Jack, I'll tell you what I'll do. You sit there and warm yourself. I'm going over to the Church to ask God what to do. I'll be back shortly.'

With that he went off and I was left sitting alone in the kitchen. He was a lovely man and I was sad to see that he could make no decision without performing some kind of rain dance in front of the altar. With as much patience as I could, I bided my time and shamelessly heedless of everything that poor Uncle Martin stood for and held dear, went to the kettle and with full knowledge and free consent, made myself another pot of tea. There was no doubt about it but that I was a very weak willed man and unless I took myself very sharply in hand within the very near future, I would only have myself to blame if I gave up the drink altogether and spent the rest of my life in the Pioneers. I know men who have gone down that slippery path and spent the rest of their days regretting it. I have often sat the night away, being a comfort to them as they slobbered in self pity about the day they took to the tea and spent the rest of their lives playing Spot the Ball and watching Nightlight instead of being out with their comrades drinking for Ireland. Some of them even got married and had children. The idle teapot is the divil's playground.

These sombre recollections were disturbed by the firm footfall in the yard as Father Coddle came back and let himself in on the kitchen door.

'That's alright, Jack,' he said calmly. 'I'll see the decent woman and the bank first thing in the morning and the documents will be signed first thing after dinner.'

'Is that what he said?' I asked, wondering if I had missed a voice from heaven which might have had something constructive to say about the runners at Punchestown.

'He said nothing,' said Father Coddle. 'I told him what I was up to and told him that if he wanted it to work out properly he better do something about it.'

I was unused to the concept of a God who could be

told what to do.

'Ring me, Father, the minute the deal is done. If I'm not at the office, try the Shelbourne Hotel. I'm often over there, minding an investment.'

'I'll be on to you, Jack, the minute the papers are signed.'

'And you'll sell to nobody until I give the word?'

'Sound. I don't like this kind of thing at all and I'd be obliged for your wise counsel.'

'Now, Father, I don't want to be greedy, but I wouldn't say "no" if you brewed up another sup of tea for I am in a state of anxiety and a sup of tea might settle me down.'

I have my father to thank for an inability to sit still for any great length of time. From the days of my childhood he gave me many the larruping on the derrier and to this very day my rear end is a tender terrain and prolonged sitting down, even in the comfort of a taxi is a sore trial to me. The tea had also made me dreadfully thirsty, and fearful of falling on evil ways, I bade the driver stop at Moate, Kilbeggan, Tyrellspass, Rochfortsbridge, Kinnegad, Enfield, Kilcock, Maynooth and Leixlip. With democratic evenhandedness, we did business in many a licensed premises, and as we neared the metropolis, my heart sang with the innocent happiness only known to those who spend their lives doing a good turn. The driver took a bad turn at Dame Street and went into Burton's window and there we sat amongst nattily tailored suits, overturned dummies and enormous shards of glass, singing in lusty chorus the full score from *The Pirates of Penzance* until the Guards arrived and told the driver that they'd do him for breaking and entering and in that way, at least, he'd keep his licence which he badly needed to earn his living. I gave a rambling account of having been kidnapped and forced to go drinking which they did not take seriously and having taken me to College Street and fired more tea into me, they thoughtfully drove me to the Shelbourne where I deemed it prudent to spend the night being good to myself after the unsettling events of the day. I knocked up, that is, I knocked on the doors of thirteen irate old bats until I found Vi's room. My heart rose again as I heard the tinkle of her girlish laughter from within and then fell heavily as I heard Delaney's boorish roar telling me to fuck off to hell out of that with myself. In a fit of pique, I resolved to do him a bad turn if ever I could and before I went asleep I knelt by my bed asking that I be given guidance in that intent.

I awoke next morning bright and early at half past eleven, feeling, as Miss Elizabeth Taylor often does, like a new man. I ordered breakfast in bed, that being, regrettably, the only commodity I seemed capable of getting in bed in those stringent times. Then I rose and showered, dressed myself with care and went out to proceed to the office, walking on foot. That latter phrase is not the pedantry it would first seem. There are those who think in their own minds, feel personally, and will on occasion cycle on bicycles. It was a mild morning, unseasonal in its clemency and I walked cheerfully along filling my lungs with the fresh blue diesel fumes from the buses, a welcome change from the damp, gloomy air of the midlands. Down along Stephen's Green I went, up past Traitor's Gate, and along past the College of Surgeons where a white man had actually been spotted in nineteen and forty six. I shed a tear at the next corner where once Mr. Cullen's Winter Garden Palace proudly stood; now no more, alas; gone like last year's Programme for Government, and now replaced by yet another monstrosity portrayed in concrete and glass, loosely spoken of as 'architecture', another monument to the speculator's greed. Up Harcourt Street I walked, feeling better with every step and ruing the days I had spent in buses and other forms of transport. God nose, it's not too much to ask that people will take the minimum amount of exercise. There are those who spend all their time encased in cars and buses, fuming furiously in the immobile traffic, sitting stunned in states of trance, with their bowels becoming sluggish, their circulation not properly circulating, breathing in nothing but fumes and farts and wondering why they feel so bad all the time. If everybody walked to work and stopped for rest here and there along the way at various public houses, the National business could proceed with an air of levity and boisterous camraderie instead of the surly, po-faced intercourse with which the sluggish conduct their affairs; V.A.T. returns not made, letters unanswered, T.V. licences not taken out and Christmas on us again, and not a damn thing got for anybody; and no letter written to Nellie in Boston after she being good enough to send on the photographs after the Saint Patrick's Day Parade. Through a labyrinth of ways I made mine, whistling snatches of Marching through Georgia through my teeth until I slowed down, transferred some weight to the left to take the corner and swung jauntily into Guinness Row.

Oh great God in heaven! Oh, sweet great fuck on wheels!

In a well ordered city,the sky is contained above the rooftops and only out in the open expanse of the countryside does it reach the ground in the distance. That was not the situation which obtained in Guinness Row that morning. An unfamiliar vista rose before me, afflicting me greatly and making me wonder if, at last, it was time to take to the tea and gallop out to Stillorgan to be dried out. The sky did run along the rooftops, as was the norm; but when it came to numbers ten, eleven, twelve and thirteen Guinness Row, it descended sharply and kissed the clouds of dust rising from the rubble of what was once the corporate headquarters of Image Erections (International) Limited, Mrs. Elizabeth McGrath's place of residence, and that essential hostelry trading as The Cart and Horse. A great sobbing rose in my chest, and I walked slowly like a man wading through a nightmare after a feed of curry consumed too late at night. The street was alive with corporation lorries and Garda vehicles with flashing blue lights. All traffic was diverted to make things utterly impossible elsewhere. Old before his time, Brannigan stood with his mouth still open with Cynthia in his arms, the broken hearted girl weeping helplessly.

'Oh, Jack, Jack. My picture was in there,' she cried.

'What the fuck is going on?' I enquired in the courteous way of one who wished to be placed in possession of the facts without delay.

Brannigan wiped a tear from his eye.

'They're saying it collapsed during the night.'

'And what about Mrs. McGrath? Did she get out alive?'

'Fuck it, Jack; isn't she the lucky woman? Isn't she gone to Teneriffe on her holidays?'

'And Christy? Is Christy alright?'

'Isn't he inside in the rubble looking for his red notebook?'

'God save and protect us all! Was anybody hurt?'

'Damn the one, thank God. They're saying that once it began to creak and groan, they got everybody out and then they knocked it to make it safe.'

'Who knocked it?'

'I don't know.'

'Oh, God, my picture, my picture.'

There was no use standing about mourning for what used to be. The only constant is change and we cannot embrace the new until we say goodbye to the old. We are but souls in transit, moving ever onward to a tomorrow ever new. But we part in pain from old familiar ways. Cynthia was very distressed and poor old Brannigan was badly shaken but bearing up bravely. It was time to take command and rally my scattered troops. It was essential to keep moral up and the hour of battle almost upon us.

'Come on,' I said, asserting control. 'We'll transfer our business to the Clinging Spittle round the corner and put ourselves in good heart. This is a terrible shock, God knows.'

'You'll get no slate there, Jack.'

'First things first. I'll squander a bit of money, for we can't stay standing about like this, with no drink inside us and we all unmanned by grief.'

A desolate trio, we wandered out of the street and

round the corner. Refugees must put in at any port they can. The Clinging Spittle was not the worst place, a resort of polished brass rails, potted plants in urns and the dreaded television set up on the top shelf, dominating the drinking with its evil eye. I gave the order and called a double up of the same, not yet being able to trust the agility of the barman and mindful of the prospect of not having a drink in front of me when I wanted it, a dreadful pass to come to.

'That's a desperate business,' remarked the barman. 'I'd have taken me oath that them houses were sound in wind and limb for another hundred years.'

'There you are, now,' said Brannigan, as philosophically as the hangman who placed the noose on the poor fellow's neck and said: 'let that be a lesson to you now'.

'Desperate,' said Cynthia, her red nose tipping above her glass of Scotch and red lemonade. 'Oh, Jack, my picture.'

'Don't worry, me poor old flower. We'll get you a new one and you won't know yourself.'

'But I've no wall to put it on.'

There was a chilling logic to that. In fact, as of that moment, the corporate enterprise known as Image Erections (International) Limited shared the same status as the oldest established, permanent, floating crap game in New York. Some headquarters had to be found and quickly. I was a monied man although not too keen on that fact being noised about in front of Brannigan and Cynthia. People can be very grasping when they know that somebody is well off. The wealthy can make very rapid friends. However, we couldn't straggle about the streets and nobody having a blind notion where to find us if they wanted their image erected.

'We'll take up our stand in the bar at the Shelbourne for the time being. When we're less pressed for time, we can look around for new offices.'

'Do they have pints there?' asked Brannigan warily.

'Big creamy ones,' I assured him, 'like the icing on a wedding cake.' Cynthia began to cry.

'I want to talk to Jack,' she sobbed. Brannigan and I were quite surprised.

'I'll go for a piss,' said Brannigan obligingly. I braced myself to fork out a few pounds for another enlargement from the *Irish Times* and a gilt frame from Quinnsworth. I wasn't too sure if the management at the Shelbourne would let us hang it in the bar.

'I haven't had my period,' Cynthia whispered, looking down into her glass. The hair stood up on the back of my neck. Oh, the hammer blows of life!

'It's the shock,' I whispered back. 'I haven't had one myself for months.'

'Are you sure you didn't come?'

'Listen, love, I'm coming and going all the time. Now settle down and have a bit of patience. Worrying always delays it and I promise you you're upsetting yourself for nothing.' I began a complicated counting backwards and forwards and resolved to read up a few women's magazines to assess the time we had left to convert Ireland before Cynthia opened up like a golf umbrella and would be unable to fulfil her assigned role — assuming at all times the worst as is the base line of all emergency planning. I put my hand in my pocket and leafed off a five pound note.

'Go down to the *Irish Times* in the morning and get yourself another picture. Get a nice frame with the change.'

She brightened a little and smiled through her tears.

'You're a good man, Jack. I wouldn't mind marrying you if I had to.'

'Let there be no loose talk of marriage, Cynthia. We'll hurl cool, keep our heads, and I'll bet you you'll want a gross of Tampax before the week is out. Here's another pound.'

In a desultory manner we assuaged our grief through the day, telling each other tales of better times and the great things we would say and do in the bright future which lay ahead when Ireland turned again to the Church and a grateful Nuncio would be plying us with money for the rest of our lives. As if on cue, the Angelus sounded from the television set and a ghastly picture of the Nativity with a moon faced madonna and a blubbery infant filled the screen.

'Ssshhh. The news,' somebody said. The usual guff which passed for headlines left us wholly disinterested until the last one was read: Minister involved in Dublin building collapse. There was no further inattention on our part, and a lot of distracting noise along the bar. We saw shots of Guinness Row just as we had left it and then the bull like features of Hughie Delaney filled the screen. He appeared to be being interviewed by an anorak holding a microphone.

'I was coming from the Forty Hours Adoration at Whitefriars Street,' Delaney muttered, grave of face, 'and I was driving up through Guinness Row. The next thing I heard this terrible groaning sound and saw the front wall of the building bulge out on to the street.' He paused here and appeared unable to go on. 'You went for help, Minister?' plied the reporter. Delaney nodded wordlessly.

'I went up to my cousin Patsy Joe McDiddle in Ranelagh. He has a wrecking crane and he came down with me. I ran in and made sure everybody was out and Patsy began to take down the front wall to make it safe.'

'Did you know, Minister, that these were preserved buildings?'

'I didn't. Sure, I didn't know the place at all. Anyway, I couldn't wait and risk someone being killed.'

'And what happened then?'

Delaney gulped.

'We had just made sure everyone was out and Patsy was making the upper part safe with his ball hammer when the whole building collapsed into the street.' He closed his eyes and shook his head. 'I never seen anything like it. It was like a bomb ....'

'Minister, it is being alleged that you had bought this building for development and some people say you knocked it down deliberately. What do you say to that?' Delaney was shaking his head firmly.

'That's totally untrue. I have not and never had any

interest, direct or indirect in any property like that. I am very hurt at these things being said and I hope that when the truth comes out, those people will give me the apology I deserve.'

'Do you know of a company called Suppository Securities?'

'Never heard of it.'

'And you have no interest in that company?'

'Never heard of it and that's as true as God is my judge.'

'And can you account for these rumours which are flying about?'

Delaney blinked and shook his head. The camera held his disappointed, unhappy face until he spoke again.

'All I can say is can you imagine the rumours if I had drove on and left the people get killed. This is just one more smear that the media are putting out to destabilise the Government.'

'The dirty bastard,' raged Brannigan.

'The whore's leavings.'

'That's the kind of fucker who called my Da a sponger.'

I ran down the counter to the barman. I had to act very quickly.

'Do you have a phone here?' I panted. He nodded his head across the room.

'Over beyond at the gents.'

With trembling hands I stuffed the slot with coins and phoned Dunfeckin 2. Father Coddle seemed a long time about coming. I had to stop him. No matter what benefit he would lose, it was unthinkable that I would do anything for Delaney after this.

'Ah, Jack, is it yourself? How are you at all, at all?'

'Listen, Father Coddle, I was having some thoughts about what I told you ....'

'Ah, did you, now? I'm only in the door this minute after being with the Solicitor. Meself and Mrs. McDermott is all fixed up. All signed, and I own the option on the land. She's only delighted, the poor woman.'

'That's good,' my voice said tonelessly as if it was

being piped in from some foreign radio station.

'Now, we'll wait in patience until we see what the Good Man Above has in store for us.'

I was crying on the phone and the tears were still in my eyes when I went back to them. I told them the truth.

'You wha'?' said Brannigan.

'You heard.'

'You're going to put that hoor's leavings in big money after what he done?' asked Cynthia. Her lip curled and her hand came up, the nails on her fingers twisting into the shape of a claw.

'It's either that or Father Coddle is left holding the can. He can't afford to. He'd be ruined. And the poor widow woman wouldn't get her money.'

'Jesus tonight!'

'But how will Delaney sell it on, if nobody else can?'

'Once the apparition takes place, Delaney will start up about an airport. He'll sell the land to the Government for twenty times the price.'

'Ah, go to hell, Jack. They're stupid, for fuck's sake, but not that stupid.'

'He'll get a valuer to put a mad price on it — for a price, of course.'

'And supposing, like, the place isn't fit for an airport, Jack?'

'Do you think that would stop them, if they'd all get their little slice under the table? If it pays them, they'd put an airport on the side of a mountain.'

Brannigan stopped shaking his head and lifted his pint. Brannigan is a thinking man.

'Begod they would,' he said. But Cynthia was still shaking her head.

'There's no way I'm going on with this. I'm not going to make money for a crowd of fucking chancers.' I didn't say anything. I didn't have to.

'Well then, me old flower,' said Brannigan slowly, 'poor Father Coddle is done down; and yer nabs above, Father Luciano will be out looking for us to give us the last sacraments sand that's a little turnup we might all be well to avoid.'

After a while even Cynthia began to see the point at issue. She stood there twisting her lip, her eyes aflame.

'I'll fucking well tell Mrs. Robinson,' she said at last.

With heavy heart and no small confusion, I walked back across the city to the Shelbourne Hotel. It was a civilised eating house with all proper facilities and I thought to spend another night there to rest myself, as the days were becoming too exciting and the man who will not take proper rest is the man who clutches his heart, goes blue in the face and goes down in a heap amidst a surging crowd of people shouting at each other to stand back and give him air. As I walked along contemplating the perversity of life which enables the evil ones to prosper and triumph as Delaney would, and the good to struggle in want, as poor Father Coddle did; a discreet toot on a horn made me turn my head to behold Monsignor Casserole's elegant vehicle sliding into the kerb beside me and, as usual, the back door swinging open in silent token of the proposition that I should enter. Lured by the prospect of further money, I stepped in and with frigid condescension, Monsignor Casserole handed over a further bundle of money. To show him I was being alert, I flicked the edges of it across the palm of my hand, tapped it on my knee and secreted it as usual close to my heart.

'I am to advise you that His Excellency is persevering in his prayerful urgency but with increasing dismay.'

'He must keep up his faith and read the papers next Monday.'

'I see. I trust he will see something more stimulating than Curly Wee. You are still consorting with Mrs. Schultz?'

'Mrs. Schultz?'

'Virginia Langley, I take it you prefer to call her.'

'Oh. I seem to run into her now and then.'

'Her mission here is to investigate your Mr. Brannigan. Tell her what she wants to know.'

'Brannigan? You are jesting, Monsignor.'

'I am not jesting and we require that she completes

her mission and returns home at the earliest time. Father Luciano says that she is a highly intelligent C.I.A. agent and her continued presence here constitutes a security risk which causes Father Luciano some concern. You will tell her what she wants to know.'

'I don't know what she wants to know. And if the idea is that she's investigating Brannigan, that's the daftest cover story I ever heard in my life.'

'Vatican Intelligence has penetrated Langley. We know why she is here. See that she is given what she wants so that she will leave.'

Chapter Ten

Isn't it bloody gas the way a man can't wake up in his bed, have his breakfast and go down to the bar for an eye opener to steady the hand without having to beat and kick his way through a crowd of thooleramawns and lachicos, hookey District Justices and politicians at the nudge, to get up near the counter and say his piece? Nothing but thimble riggers and butter drummers, party yesmen and beef barons codding the Department; all clustered round Hughie Delaney and he winking and nodding and sucking his pint, and the Gay Byrne Hour not even over. God nose it's a great little country just the same. I recoiled in dismay and then found that Brannigan and Cynthia were ensconced at a discreet corner table. If there's one thing I insist upon, and that's the staff getting in early for nothing can be done until the team is on the field and ready to make a go of the day.

Brannigan was behind the paper and Cynthia was sipping her Scotch and red lemonade. There are those who might think that putting red lemonade in good whiskey is a dreadful thing to do and that any girl who would do such a thing wasn't, God help her, up to much; but I was inclined to let it pass; although if it were Irish she was putting it in, I could see that grave moral considerations would arise. Howandever, live and let live. The Shelbourne was a pleasant place, if you ignored the gobshites at the bar, but the persistent refusal to run a slate was a drawback. Good money had to be paid out on delivery and it's very hard to build up a substantial cash balance with that class of thing going on. On the other hand, there was a very efficient paging and telephone system, the barmen were first rate and wouldn't leave a man in drought and at least we were spared Mrs. McGrath and her vulgar pleasantries. By the mercy of God, I caught the barman's eye and within moments I had two doubles in front of me to open the bidding and the barman instructed to hold himself on standby, poised to spring at the twitch of an eyebrow.

'Do you know where the hoor was yesterday?' asked Brannigan. I did not know where the hoor was yesterday but I didn't worry because I knew I would be told.

'Below in the Four Courts and he perjuring a hole in a pot for the afternoon.'

'And could the wiggy-wiggies not get anything out of him?'

'No. Claimed privilege and quoted the Official Secrets Act.'

'And could the Judge not nail him?'

'The Judge was asleep and then he woke up and ruled that he was not asleep.'

'That's like the Pope declaring that he is infallible. Was he infallible when he made that declaration?'

'Desperate,' said Cynthia, who was far more interested in getting to the bottom of her glass and keeping a venomous eye on Hughie Delaney with a look which would scorch granite.

Ireland is an interesting country. The Judges and the politicians who pride themselves on being the fearless guardians of the public weal are as often as not engaged in a tacit conspiracy to prevent the truth coming out. By manipulation of parliamentary procedure and the rules of evidence, an enthralling game is played out. For this public entertainment — and God knows we need the odd laugh — they are cosseted and pampered and keep themselves in eminent isolation from the public they purport to serve but privately despise. Adept at playing the system which they themselves put in place and change when it suits them, they arrange generous pensions for each other and the various perks and privileges denied to those they are supposed to serve. Any scandal which comes to public knowledge is inevitably brought out by the efforts of the Fourth Estate who enjoy no perks and privileges at all, and for this reason the politicos and the Courts spend a lot of time trying to curtail the work of the journalists, lest the game become less enjoyable. It's all an exciting little diversion which the public enjoy and which keeps their minds off the possibility of rising up and horsewhipping these effete layabouts from their places of privilege and demanding that they do an honest day's work. No one seriously expected that the Judicial Enquiry into the workings of An Bord Meow would reveal anything startling except irrelevant little malpractices which would leave the Minister unscathed. For all that, it was pleasant to pass the morning listening to Brannigan retailing the news out over the top of his paper, pausing to lift his pint and draw it in behind the wall of newsprint from time to time.

'Do you know what the hoor said?'

'No.'

'That he was a man of integrity and that he had been very hurt by the campaign of villification being waged against him by the media.'

'Which, again, is like the Church talking about love and compassion.'

'Aye, the fuckers.'

'Desperate.'

I became aware that Delaney had detached himself from his coterie and was standing at my elbow. He nodded surreptitiously to the door. I braced myself with a stiff swallow and followed him out.

'I hear,' he murmured out of the corner of his mouth, 'that the hour is nigh.'

I was noncommital but mentioned that I knew of a tract of land which could be bought for a certain figure. With some private glee I made it clear that the land was snipe grass and callows. The bull head of him shot up indignantly.

'Are you fucking joking me or what?' he enquired in

his best Ministerial tones, 'and it pure bloody bogland?'

'Over two thousand acres, Hughie. All in a piece. Ideal for the main runway. Jesus, Hughie, can't you see it? Big runway with vasi lights; Delaney International.'

'Not at that kind of money. Sure, Jasus, d'ye see, that's about ten times its value. It would put me at full stretch.'

'If it's the only place for the main runway, you'll flog it to the Government for twice that.' Like everybody else I was aware of Government policy of blithely paying prices far above the official valuation and I could see no reason why the practice which obtained in the little seaside town of Blackrock could not apply in the pleasant rural hamlet of Dunfeckin, and bugger the Comptroller and Auditor General.

'Ah, g'way outa that, will ya. Do you think I'm pure gone in the head.'

'That's O.K., Hughie. I promised I'd give you first option.'

He meditated in his calculations while my heart stood still. Brinksmanship is what they call it in informed circles.

'Is that your last word?' he said at last.

'It is,' I said without a blink. His beefy face paled a little, he rubbed the back of his neck with a shovel-like hand but the greedy look of the pig at the trough never left his eyes. He made an interesting study of the cute hoor thinking like a cute hoor.

'Alright so,' he said quickly after a long pause. Whatever devious scheme had occurred to him, he seemed anxious to proceed. 'When do you want the money? I can let you have a cheque this afternoon.'

'No cheque, thanks, Hughie. A bank draft made payable to P. Coddle.' The man who would take a Ministerial personal cheque should be heavily sedated, confined to bed and caringly counselled by skilled psychiatrists.

'A bank draft? For the whole thing?'

'Yes, Hughie.'

'And not a bloody line in writing?'

'And what better way to have it, Hughie? Sure, you know nothing about it.'

He gave me a quick, crafty look, not unmixed with some dawning respect.

'Jasus, you'd make a grand party man, so you would.' He eyed round the lobby, for the politician's eyes are always moving to see who is looking at him. He nestled closer. 'Now, Jack,' he whispered, 'where is it to be?'

'Bank draft first, Hughie.'

'Jasus Christ, man; do you not trust me at all? Sure, if I wanted to, couldn't I bide me time until the balloon goes up and then buy it meself?'

'I honestly don't know what you're talking about, but then wouldn't I have the land sold to the others?'

'The others?'

'You're not the only one in the running.' He swung around angrily and was doubtless soothed by my engaging smile.

'Right so,' he said at last. 'I'll drop it into you here during the afternoon.'

'Good enough. I'll do no business with the others until three o'clock.'

'You have no fucking integrity. None at all. Wheeling and dealing all over the place, so you are. I'm very disappointed in you, Jack.'

'Ah, Hughie; don't be hard on me. We all have to turn a shilling.'

'Cynthia was smouldering when I got back to the table.

'That's the fucker who called my Da a sponger,' she said, rebuking me for the company I had been keeping. 'By God, I'll settle the big bastard yet.'

'That you may,' I said, thinking only that Father Coddle's faith would shortly be rewarded.

I woke slowly in an idyllic dream, with the rose glow of the bedside lamp bathing my eyes restfully and the erotic tang of Vi's perfume wafting in my nostrils. Be life long or short, I have been through a peak experience and whether death came from a bullet in the skull from

Father Luciano or a gentle going out into night, I would not die wondering. Vi's tawny hair fell down across my face as she cradled me, her warm breasts full against me, and the Private Member asleep in its satiation, probably never needing to stir again for many the long octave. She sat up on one elbow; gazing down at me, stroking my hair and tracing the lines of my face with her forefinger.

'Did the earth move for you?' she asked softly.

'All the chinamen jumped together.'

'Hey now. You're some performer. Sure ringa-ding-thing.'

'Yeah. All the women tell me that.'

For some moments I lost myself in her great gazing depths of azure blue.

'Hi there, Mrs. Schultz,' I said mischievously, ever the one for the boyish prank when least expected. She gazed unblinkingly down at me and then a slow, self-conscious smile crept over her face.

'If you ever meet him, don't tell Colonel Schultz I've been in bed with you.'

'Who is Colonel Schultz?'

'My Station Controller. He runs me. He's also my husband.'

If there's one class of person we can all get on quite well without, it's the mean spirited, spiteful, selfish bastard commonly known as the irate husband. I wouldn't give them time of day. The man who won't share the good things of life that providence has been gracious enough to bestow, doesn't deserve them in the first place and he would do well to remind himself that what God gives with one hand, he can take away with the other. There is a terrible poverty of mind, a self serving acquisitiveness in those who clasp their possessions to their bosoms and won't allow other people share in their good fortune. God nose, we're supposed to be a Christian country where every man is a brother; we're supposed to pull together and give a neighbour a day when he's at the hay, and there can be no place amongst us for the hard faced and heartless who won't place his gifts at the disposal of others. It is my considered opinion, and some will find the insight an incisive one, that locking wives up in kitchens with squalling platoons of sticky children is directly responsible for the epidemic of tea drinking which afflicts the country at the moment. You've heard me say it in this House before and I make no apology for saying it again; that until we buckle down and grasp the nettle of the tea drinking — and this means, inter alia, allowing the women have their bit on the side — we have as much chance of solving the problems which bedevil us as getting Garrett Fitzgerald to stop talking. I'll leave it at that, for I suppose there's no point in going on and bloody on about it, but I do hope I won't have to mention the matter again.

'Hey, Vi, what's your interest in Brannigan?'

She looked at me coolly.

'You're very well informed, Jack. Am I blown?'

''Fraid so. Time to come in from the cold.'

'Gee, that's a pity. You've got a nice little island here and that's for sure. Brannigan is trying to smuggle in some of our gunships and we can't locate the source on our side. Who is Sergeant Rickenbacker?'

'A sixteen year old boy from Booterstown with an American accent born on the Fourth of July.'

'You're kidding!'

'I kid you not. It's all a game, Vi. We never stop playing games in this country.'

'Prove it.'

'No problem. You can meet Brannigan and Thady and hear them at work. It's pretty realistic.'

'Aw shit. You telling me I've been here for nothing all this time?'

My hand crept affectionately along the smooth rounded thigh which lay against my stomach.

'I wouldn't like you to think that, Vi.' She kept shaking her head and laughing sadly to herself.

'Hey now. Well ain't that something else?'

The following day I rang Father Coddle to make sure that he had got the post and that all was well. He was very moved and emotional with gratitude, and wholly unable to comprehend the amount involved.

'But, God bless us, Jack, how did you do it? Dear, dear, dear, I didn't think there was that much money in the whole country. How did you do it at all?'

'Ah, now, Father, pure chance. We mustn't question the ways of God.'

'Well, that's as true as I'm standing here. I'm going to split it with Mrs. McDermott, the poor woman and I'll settle the odd bit here and there — there's great hardship in the Parish. And I've a bit for yourself, Jack; and no man more entitled to it.'

'No, Father,' I heard my voice say, 'I wouldn't touch a shilling of it. It's a matter of conscience.' That just goes to show that salient phone calls should never be made when a man is half drunk.

'Ah, dear, dear, Jack, you're a terrible man, yourself and your conscience.'

'Leave a gin and tonic for me in every pub in Dunfeckin.'

Don't talk to me about Cornelius Ryan and The Longest Day, I've been there. I'll never forget that Sunday we spent in the hayloft waiting for dusk. Brannigan was fidgeting like a badger in a bag and complaining that he had nothing to drink, and Cynthia, in her Virgin Mary outfit, was scratching like a hen in a yard, complaining that the hay was making her itchy. I shared both complaints; a raging thirst as the day wore on and an infuriating skin irritation from the same hay, and no smoking lest we leave cigarette ends after us and give the game away. You could bottle the tension between us and sell it as Worcester sauce. At one point we were damn near to saying the Rosary to pass the time.

Shortly after midday, a spate of bad language and bucolic shouting was heard and when Brannigan looked out covertly from the slit window, he reported that two teams of thooleramawns had taken the field to play a match. One or two cars had arrived as well but it was by no means anything like a crowd; being, apparently, a small rural disturbance between two parishes. Cynthia, bored out of her head by now but still looking most celestial in her costume, put her eye to the other slit to observe the play.

'Jasus, Jack, there's more than twenty of them out there and they've only one football between the lot of them.'

'Yeah, that's how they do it.'

We had left Thady in a pub in Dunfeckin where he could play a game of Star Wars for the day and I gave him fifty pee and told him to buy himself all the fizzy orange he wanted.

'But, surely, if they had a ball each; they could all run up and down and score all the goals they like.'

I looked at her with awakening interest. The girl had a point. The practice of playing these games with only one ball between all the players leads to nothing else but breaches of the peace, unruly behaviour, and, often enough, mutual assaults contrary to Common Law and the various Statutes provided. An arrangement whereby each player had a ball each would mean that everybody could score — willy nilly — and over a timed period it would be a matter of seeing which team could score the most. I could see at once that football hooliganism on the pitch, which usually made anything on the terraces look like Come Dancing, would be a thing of the past.

'Begod, you're a bright girl and no mistake.'

'I think I'll write to Mrs. Robinson about it.'

Brannigan looked at me and I looked at Brannigan. It was essential to keep her mind on the business at hand and we didn't want any distracting conversations about Mrs. Robinson or, most particularly, anything which would rouse her fury against Hughie Delaney and throw her into a fit of artistic hysterics before the performance. We had had more than enough trouble coming down in the car when she threatened to down tools because Hughie was going to make a few bob on the day and if we hadn't got into a place in Kinnegad and fired a few Vodkas into her to relax her, I'd say she would have walked off the set. She couldn't get it out of her head that Delaney had wrecked the house down on her picture. However the little interregnum calmed her down and I was happy that we might look forward to a polished performance and possibly a great one. I was right about that.

As the sun began to slant towards the west — exactly the way it does in Dublin — I decided to hold a pre-count-down conference. We wanted no messing and it was Brannigan who put that idea in my head.

'Why is the Government like a two-bit hoor?' said he, a smart aleckey grin spreading over his face. I didn't know and Cynthia didn't know.

'A new cock-up every day,' said Brannigan, pleased with himself.

'I don't get that,' Cynthia said.

'Don't mind that,' said Brannigan, 'you will.' The dirty blaggard and we about to do a stroke. No one can expect any luck if that's the kind of smut and dirt they talk and I just felt that we can all get on quite well without that class of thing.

'Right,' said I, 'we'll have a last run through. Cynthia, over by the wall. Brannigan, you'll keep observation through the slit. I'll be here with the light. Now, Cynthia, just pretend you're standing at the opening. I'll be here, out of sight with the light, where you can see me without turning your head. Right?'

We took up our positions. My hands were beginning to shake and Brannigan began to have that worn look he used to have in the old days when we were at the Law and he used to read the file of Fallopian Tubes (Ireland) Limited. Only Cynthia was showing any signs of confidence.

'O.K., Cynthia; in the dark. Action.'

She drew herself up demurely, joined her hands, and held her head erect.

'Bow the head, ever so slightly. You'll be looking down on them. Now, a teeny, weeny, gentle smile.'

She was perfection. Even Brannigan stopped chewing his lip.

'Terrific, terrific. Now, Cynthia; pretend I'm bringing up the light, slowly, wowly, slowly, wowly; that's it, hold it. Hold it. Terrific.'

She was carved like a statue. Under lights it would have been magic.

'Now. When I move my finger ....'

I moved my finger. Her eyes never strayed towards me.

'I am the Immaculate Conception,' she said. Though she played her voice down, it was confident and with bell like clarity.

'Keep holding it. Lovely. Lovely.' Then I moved my finger again.

'Listen to the Holy Father! Listen to the Bishops! Listen to the Priests!' It wasn't just a performance; it was a tour-de-force, whatever that might be.

'O.K., Cynthia, just hold it there. That's all you have to say but we'll hold you in place for a few minutes and then I'll fade down the light.'

'What will we do then?' said Brannigan, one eye closed and the other glued to the slot.

'We run like fuck. If we meet anybody, just act excited and ask them where the apparition is.'

'And, Jasus, Jack, what if they rush us when we're here?'

'Rush us? Look, me old flower, with Cynthia playing as well as that, they'll be rooted to the ground.'

They were. The afternoon went cloudy gold in the sky and as twilight came on, the football players shouted their final 'Ah fuck you' across the field and the whistle went. Cynthia was in place, fully controlled; and with trembling hands, I switched on the flood lamp and began to bring up the dimmer. Slowly, shimmeringly in the filters of blue, Cynthia was transformed. She ceased to be human and became an incandescent, ethereal being. Had I drink taken or not been there to see the rehearsal, I would have fallen to my knees, my beseeching hands raised over my head. She stood there in heavenly brightness, immobile and wondrous.

'What are they doing?' I whispered to Brannigan. I could see him pressing his eye to his peep hole.

'Jasus, Jack, old son,' he grunted slowly, 'you were

right. Every man jack of them is stuck to the ground, and, fuck me, they're going down on their knees.' He stood back and rubbed his eye and then went back to his observations.

'I declare to God, but there's other people coming and they're dumbstruck. There isn't a bloody word out of the whole lot of them. I think you've frightened the shit out of them.'

I had a star on my hands; a star to direct and control and fill with confidence.

'Hold it right there, Cynthia; just smile. You're doing great.'

I need not have worried. No actress was ever in more secure command of her part. My mind went back to that first meeting with Father Coddle in the Fart and Arse, that sinister encounter with Monsignor Casserole and the inspiring visit to the Nuncio and all the weeks of tireless planning and rehearsal and I knew that here we were and despite all the problems we were achieving the impossible. Cynthia was a model of artistic patience. I could detect no strain or stress in her.

'Jesus tonight,' said Brannigan, 'would you believe there's a crowd of them there already?'

'What are they doing?'

'All hands down on the knees and the mouths open like the pigeon holes in a post office. Bejasus, they'll set the place on fire yet. Candles, if you please.'

I looked up at Cynthia and moved my finger.

'Now Cynthia!'

A beatific smile broke across her face.

'I am the Immaculate Conception,' she said. Her voice rang across the field like the music of angels. We could hear a reverential sigh going up from the crowd like a high wind. I moved my finger again.

'Now, Cynthia!'

'Listen to the Holy Father! Listen to the Bishops! Listen to the Priests!' Another great sigh rose from outside.

'O.K., baby, hold it. Hold it. I'm bringing down the lights.'

My hand was sweating as I grasped the dimmer switch and almost imperceptibly Cynthia began to fade away. Slowly the loft filled with a stygian blackness. I reached for Cynthia's hand and guided her back from the opening.

'Where are you, Brannigan?' I whispered.

I heard a rustle in the straw.

'I'm over here and I never seen anything like it in my life. There's more of them coming in cars. Lights all over the place. Jasus, it's like the All Ireland in the middle of the night.'

'O.K. Let's get the fuck out of here.'

'Ah, Jasus, I don't know. Sure that was only the matinee. Can't we wait and give them another go. Midnight movie, like.'

'No way. No goddam way. Quit when we're ahead.'

'Oh goodie,' said Cynthia. 'I'd love to do it again.'

'No, Cynthia.'

'Well, I'm staying here and doing it. It's great fun.'

'Sure, fuck it, Jack, what harm would it be? She's right. Give them a bit of value.'

A coldness began to creep over me as I groped my way over to where the slit showed against the night sky. I put my eye to it and gasped. The whole field seemed to be a moving carpet of candle light, flickering and dancing in the darkness. Away in the distance the bobbing headlamps of cars seemed to be converging from all points of the compass. We were into something far beyond our dreams. Like a night tide coming on the shore, the murmuring of organised prayer rose and fell. And I was the producer and director of the biggest show I had ever seen. I gave myself to the memory of Sam Goldwyn again to ask for guidance.

'We'll wait for an hour or two,' announced Brannigan, 'and we'll give them a late show before we go.'

'Wait a minute, now; I'm in charge of this.'

'Ah, fuck off, Jack.'

'Yes Jack. You're a right old begrudger, so you are.'

'You're the pair that can fuck off. You'll have no show without the flood light.'

'Well then,' said Cynthia, 'I'm going to go to the window and sing "Here's to you, Mrs. Robinson".'

After about three hours sitting there in the hay, trembling with the tension, a clattering high pitched wine drowned out the noise of the prayers. It came from afar, approached rapidly and thundered over our heads with a great swishing of rotors.

'That's Charlie,' said Brannigan authoritatively. 'I bet you Ciaran is driving him.' His voice muffled as if he had put his eye to the peep hole again. 'Flood lights, bejasus. I'd say it's Kenny Live. Begod, fair play to you, Cynthia, this is a great turnout altogether.'

'What time is it?' I asked dully.

'Time for the second house. Up there, Cynthia, love, and give it to them.'

It was time to reassert command.

'O.K., O.K. Get yourselves together. Now, we're going to give this our best shot. The greatest show ever. Now, Cynthia, the exact same thing again. Are you O.K.?'

'And why wouldn't I? Amn't I rearing to go?'

'O.K., give me your hand. Brannigan, keep watch.'

'Don't you fret, me ould son. I wouldn't miss it for a win on the Lottery.'

I guided Cynthia to the opening and felt my way back to where I had the flood lamp fixed on its cradle.

'Right. Shut up everyone. Curtain up. Action, Cynthia. You O.K.?'

'Go on, Jack, for Jasus sake. I'm ready.'

My hand was slippery against the control as I brought up the dimmer and the bulb glowed under the filter. A ghostly illumination started at Cynthia's feet as with a superb touch, I brought up the light slowly. Any misgivings that Cynthia had become over excited were groundless. She was manifested slowly, her head bowed perfectly under the blue veil, her cloak falling round her, stirring imperceptibly in the breeze. Once again, it was a scene from another world. The humming of the prayers fell away and an awful stricken silence came down on the throng.

'Hold it, Cynthia, hold it. I'll give you the sign in a

moment.' I could hardly credit that this poor, inexperienced Dublin girl could possess such a presence. I moved my finger.

Slowly, she spoke.

'I am the Immaculate Conception.'

It was even more perfect than the first time. If silence could deafen, we were deafened.

'Hold it, Cynthia, hold it, kid. Just a few minutes.'

It was no trouble to her. She was superb. And just at that moment, a hoarse, bull-like roar rose from the front of the crowd.

'Hail Queeeeeeen of Heaveeeeeeen ....'

'Jesus,' said Brannigan, 'It's Hughie Delaney and he up in front starting a hymn.' Horrified, I raised my eyes to Cynthia. She reverently lifted her joined fingertips to cover her mouth.

'That's the fucker who called my Da a sponger,' she hissed.

'Don't mind the bastard,' I whipped back. 'Hold your position. Stay in character. Cynthia!'

The angelic smile never left her face. Slowly her hands parted and she began to extend her arms in a grand embrace.

'No, Cynthia, no! For Christ's sake, Cynthia.'

The veil slipped back from her head and she raised it proudly and erectly. With a heroic effort I controlled my bowels.'

'No, Cynthia! No! For fuck's sake, Cynthia!'

The beatific smile broadened across her face until it was alive with pride, joy and a great welcome. Like a great clarion, a trumpet of triumph, all out across the lands of Dunfeckin and beyond with passionate intensity, her voice rang forth.

'I am of Ireland! Come dance with me in Ireland!'

Chapter Eleven

I'm persecuted with Solicitors' letters from the man in the Long Mile Road looking for his backpack and the flood light. The Guards have them below in Moate and I'm afraid of my bloody life to open the post for the dread of a Civil Bill because those things don't come cheap and that man isn't inclined to let the hare sit and say nothing. And not another shilling, of course, from the canonical crowd above in the Park. Put not your trust in princes.

I don't remember getting down off the loft but that's hardly surprising given the shock of the whole thing. I'd say I ran a parish or two before the others caught up with me.

'You're a nice fucking article,' said Brannigan.

'You're one right hoor, Jack, running off like that.'

'I thought you were ahead of me. I was only looking for a pub.'

We were on some backroad and the glow of the television lights was still in the sky behind us. We could hear shouting and car horns blowing. Ahead were the lights of Dunfeckin. It must have been about three a.m. but it might as well have been angelus time on a fair day. It was essential to get some drink into us and show a bit of consideration for poor Thady who had been waiting all day. Late, or early maybe, as it was, it seemed that the whole of Ireland had converged on Dunfeckin on the head of the Nine o'clock news, and every pub and sheebeen in the place was sweating with barmen pulling pints and sawing off mountains of sandwiches. Poor Thady was jammed in the thick of a pulsating crowd, and he drunk out of his head like everyone else. It's a dreadful state of affairs when you can't leave a young man with a game of Star Wars to entertain him without coming back to find that he had broken his Pledge and was passing himself off as Dustin Hoffman and the American talk out of him. In the latter end we fought our way to the bar and I, relying falsely on the Church keeping me plied in money was actually paying for all the rounds. After a while, despite the seriousness of our plight and the threat of Father Luciano's vengeance, we had enough down to view the situation in a less than critical light. Nobody passed a bit of notice on us as strangers were many that night and there were several buckos there in turbans from the County Hospital and Chinamen who had come to Trinity to learn Irish. As far as we could overhear, most people believed that the apparition was the work of Satan and that it was the appearance of Hughie Delaney which had evoked him. What view of the matter was held above in the Nunciature we neither knew or cared at the time; none of us dreaming that we would care most acutely in due course.

'Well, that's fucked that,' I said with some bitterness.

'Sure, what about it,' said Brannigan airily, 'wasn't it the grand bit of crack while it lasted?'

'Desperate,' said Cynthia, taking off her shoes and holding them up for my inspection. 'I'll be looking for a few bob for these, Jacko, old son.'

'And there's the small matter of the mother's cloak and veil,' said Brannigan. 'I'd say five hundred pounds would cover the lot including the night's hire.'

'You can't blame me for that, Brannigan. I wasn't the one who stuffed them into a bush.'

'No? Did you expect her to be parading round wearing them and the crowd screaming for blood? Five hundred, Jack.'

'Oh, alright. I'll get you out a cheque in a few days.'

'I mightn't be here in a few days. Cash will do. Now.'

He held out his hand, there and then, with half of Ireland looking on.

'Brannigan, you're joking.'

'*Now*, Jack. Did you ever get a puck in the gob?'

Between the Shelbourne and various petty miscellaneous outlay I was down to almost nothing, but the heartless bastard never took his eye off me until I had counted it out.

There was something else out. Cynthia's hand.

'What's wrong with you, love?'

'Me hair is ruined, me dress is ruined and me shoes is ruined. Tell you what, Jacko. Five hundred and we'll call it quits.'

'And bejasus, we won't! Breach of contract. To damages for fucking up a good show. Counterclaim five hundred pounds. Setoff. We're quits this minute. Case dismissed. Notice to Fuck Off to be filed.'

'Jack, I'm waiting.'

'Cynthia!'

'Oh, alright then. I'll be on *The Sunday Tribune* in the morning.'

Tears came to my eyes as I counted it off. I was a fiver short and they wouldn't believe me until I turned out my pockets.

'I never thought you'd do this to me,' I said, 'after all we went through together.'

'Jesus, Brannigan, wipe me nose; I'm nearly crying.'

I don't understand it. You can trust people, confide in them, lead them to great things and they'll all stand with you as long as everything is going well. Then, the slightest little hitch, a moment of miscue, the merest reverse of fortune and over the hill they've gone, fleeing like hirelings.

'You'll be scrubbers all your life,' I said, 'no breadth of vision.' For one moment I thought Brannigan had taken me seriously. His face went green and he swallowed hard and seemed to have unusual difficulty in breathing. I followed his raised eyes into the face of Father Luciano. Cynthia's face didn't go green. It was green already. Father Luciano didn't seem upset or anything like that. Just icy cold. He bent over us and placed his hands on our shoulders, like an avuncular pastor tending his flock. I remembered I had never heard him speak before.

'The door to the yard is just behind me. Walk out in single file.' He smiled like ice settling on the window pane of a morgue. 'We don't want to upset anyone here, do we?'

For the second time that night I wet my pants. It was hot and cold at the same time and I thought that I would get chilblains until I remembered I wouldn't live long enough to get chilblains. I looked at Cynthia and Cynthia looked at me. Then I looked at Brannigan and Brannigan looked at me. Then Brannigan looked at Cynthia and Cynthia looked at Brannigan. In the hundred years we took to walk out to the yard, we all did that several times. I was never more sober in my life. There was a light drizzle swirling under the yard lamp but Father Luciano indicated we might all be better off in the shadows. Quite matter-of-factly he pulled a gun from his pocket and I knew from watching too much television that the bulky bit of hardware at the muzzle was a silencer.

'Now we'll all say the Act of Contrition together,' he said pleasantly enough, 'and then we'll accept God's holy will. It will be quite painless; a headshot at this range usually is.' He almost smiled. 'There is no need to keep your hands up. Join them.'

'Glory be to the Father ... and to ....' I said. I never had more difficulty making my tongue move in my life.

'That's not the Act of Contrition, you fucking ejit.' Brannigan stammered.

'Father, I was absent the day they did that at school,' Cynthia said. The poor girl had had far too much to drink and I doubt if she knew what was going on.

Then from somewhere behind, like a sizzling whiplash, Vi spoke.

'Drop the gun, Chino, or I'll blow your fucking testicles across the block.'

Slowly she emerged into the light which glinted on a

natty little fowling piece in her hand, set fair to blow a hole in Luciano's forehead. He was very mannerly. He inclined his head resignedly and nonchalantly handed the gun to her butt first.

'We meet again, Dorothy, or should I say, Vi, or 4711. I had hoped you had gone home.'

Coldly, Vi tossed her hair back out of her eyes.

'Once we heard that VAT 0069 had come to Ireland, we wanted to know what you were up to. We didn't like losing Calvi. That wasn't very nice of you, Chino.'

We stood there trembling. We were obviously overhearing a dispassionate business discussion between two professionals from rival firms. I was wondering when we would hear a little plop and see the little crimson hole splatter over his eyes. But he nodded understandingly enough.

'Ah yes; I thought that Uncle Sam mightn't like that. Maxwell too, of course.'

'Desperate,' said Cynthia. I think Brannigan was wetting his pants too. I cannot speak for Cynthia but at least I no longer had the money to fork up for a new pair of knickers.

'Very unfriendly, Chino. Don't let it happen again.' She nodded towards us. 'These guys are friends of mine. If anything ever happened to them we'd find you and mail you back to Rome, finger by finger, toe by toe. Do you know how long it takes a man to die when there's a starving rat caged against his balls?'

Father Luciano nodded again. He seemed to be familiar with the concept she had mentioned. Casually, he glanced at his watch.

'I think I'd better go,' he said drily. 'I've a plane to catch in the morning.' He bowed slightly and turned to leave.

'Goodbye, Chino. Stay off my patch in future.' She watched coldly as Father Luciano walked slowly across the yard and out the gate. Then she followed him and stayed watching from the gate, gun in hand, until we heard a car drive off. I wanted to say something to her but my tongue was welded to the roof of my mouth.

Then she turned, glanced at us, nodded slightly and was gone.

We stood as if cemented in place for about half an hour. Then Brannigan said:

'Who's yer one, Jack?'

* * *

Christmas is a dreadful time, said Patrick Kavanagh, it brings out the bollocks in everyone. I agree. Provided the Guards were up from College Street at the table in the corner, you might get a drink after hours at the corner of Fitzwilliam Street but that apart, Christmas is hard for a man on his own and on the man on his own, other things can get very hard as well.

I got a little card from Father Coddle saying that he had said Mass for my intentions. I wish he wouldn't do that. God must have hit the crossbar because as Christmas came on, things went from bad to worse.

When I checked at the Shelbourne, I found that Vi had not alone left but they seemed to have no record at all of a Vi Langley or a Dorothy Schultz who, to my certain knowledge, had stayed there for months. I rang directory enquiries and got put through on an international call to C.I.A. Headquarters at Langley Virginia and asked to speak to her. There was a very friendly, obliging girl on the switch who told me to hold on and next thing a Colonel Cyrus Schultz came on the line, called me a son-of-a-bitch and told me that if I ever rang his wife again, he'd personally fly to Ireland in person (which is the best way to do it) and bust my ass. I was even more lonely after that. You couldn't walk the pavements without being obstructed every inch of the way by furclad South County matrons, neighing and braying at each other in their Killiney accents and blocking the way with their candy striped parcels and their enormous bums. You couldn't go into a shop or a pub that they weren't playing 'Sleighride' or Bing Crosby singing 'White Christmas' which is the kind of thing that brings on the dry gawks in me; wrist up against the wall, legs apart and shoes well back, and just nothing; nothing at all, heave after heave. You couldn't lean up against the bar for a quiet one without having the place invaded by office parties; drunken yuppies who didn't know how to drink and little streels of dowdy office girls who'd be running into Sylvia Meehan in the morning whinging that they didn't get their bottoms pinched all night long. With Brannigan gone, it was difficult to keep up with the news although I did hear on television that the Papal Nuncio, Archbishop Luigi Castrato Cojones had been recalled to Rome but, not being privy to Church affairs, I never discovered why.

I think the Brannigan business hurt most of all.

One night Cynthia said: 'Jack, Jack, everything is alright. I got it this morning.'

'Didn't I tell you not to worry,' I said, 'but we'd want to be more careful in future; that's what the airline pilots call a reportable incident, a near miss.' I had been doing some very deep thinking for some time, considering this and that and where my life was going or not going and I said to her;

'I think we should get married.'

'Oh, Jack,' Cynthia said.

'Fuck it, Cynthia, I don't see anything to laugh about,' I was speaking in a most earnest vein and couldn't see why this should evoke an outburst of levity. So she put her hand on mine and told me that Brannigan and herself were flying out to Lourdes for Christmas and getting married there. It will be a long bloody time before I ever speak to Brannigan again and I'll tell him that when I'm not speaking to him again.

I suppose there's a bright side to everything. Hughie Delaney was declared bankrupt and had to give up his Dail seat and his Ministry. The Taoiseach said that a dedicated public representative and a man of integrity had been hounded to his destruction.

One night in the very mouth of Christmas I betook myself down the town and got very drunk. There's drunkenness and drunkenness in it, but, as Vi would have said, this was pure goddam ringa-ding drunk. As the evening wore on I saw or thought I saw a half decent looking woman at the bar and I laid my chat on her because as every drink went down she began to look better and better, and she had this fascinating way of sitting on a stool and hoisting up her skirt to prevent it from getting out of shape. With suave suavity, I lured her with my silken tongue and wily ways and the job was right, if you can understand my way of putting things, which she appeared to. It was a condition of the contract that I would spend the night at her place; and I thought, thank God, any port in a storm and sure wouldn't it put down one of the lonely nights of Christmas.

When we were finally thrown out into the street, with nothing but cats elongating themselves in and out of the railings, and all the buses long abed, she rubbed her hands briskly and pulled her coat up round her ears. Do you know what she said?

'That's the hardy one!'

I swear to God every word of this is true.